Misadventure and Murder in Mistletoe

Mistletoe Treasures Book 4

By

Ronna M. Bacon

Verses

Isaiah 41:10. So do not fear, for I am with you; do not be dismayed, for I am your God. I will strengthen you and help you; for I will uphold you with my righteous right hand.

Table of Contents

Prologue

The woman straightened her jacket and then reached for her small bag and purse. She was leaving and not looking back, she decided. She didn't want what she was leaving here.

She walked from the room, her heels clicking on the tiled floor, avoiding the elevator, instead taking the stairs. She signalled for a taxi, heading for the hotel room she had been staying in, telling the taxi to wait. She gathered her belongings and headed back down, finding another taxi to take her to another hotel, where she found the vehicle she had left there the week before. She tossed the ticket on the windshield and climbed in, driving away, not looking back, not caring about what she had left behind her.

The nurse paused in the hospital room, not seeing the woman, seeing the gown crumpled on the bed, and looked back to check the room number. It was the right room, but the woman had fled. She turned, her steps taking her to find the charge nurse, consternation on her face. She looked down at the little bundle in her arms, sound asleep, a beautiful little girl with auburn hair and green eyes, abandoned by her mother.

Days went by and the mother was not found. Police detectives could not trace her, as she was not from that town. Inquiries went out but returned with no response.

The baby girl grew, placed in a loving foster home at just one week of age, her foster parents adopting her before she was much older. She was loved by all of them, a bright happy child, who still felt a shame that she had been abandoned through no fault of her own.

She grew, her faith in God unshakable. She just knew somewhere, someone did really belong to her and that God would bring her to them at some point.

She didn't see the dark shadows hanging over her head or that of her family. Shadows that spelt doom and death.

Chapter 1

*S*hrugging deeper into his jacket collar, Simon Gardner pulled his toque down further over his ears, his eyes scanning the woods around him, watching for the armed assailant they had been warned was in the area of the local hiking trails. He really didn't want to be out there, he had other things he had planned to do on his Saturday off, but when the Mistletoe police chief had put out a call for help to the county force, Simon had been contacted. He had agreed to help, since Mistletoe was his town even though he worked for the county force. He listened to the crackling voices on his radio and then walked forward, the sun reflecting off the snow and causing him to reach for his sunglasses.

He sighed. It was going to be a long day, he thought. He mentally shook his head. Not the right attitude, now is it, Lord, he asked. I guess I'm just getting tired of this, of hunting for people and worrying about my fellow officers and civilians getting hurt. I'm feeling burnt out and is this Your way of directing me to something else?

He paused as he heard a soft voice and spun trying to find the source before he frowned and then walked forward, stopping in his tracks, surprise colouring his face.

A lady was laying on the ground, her elbows planted on the blanket she had placed underneath her, her hiking boot clad feet crossed at the ankles. Simon leaned to the side, a frown turning to a half-smile as he saw the camera in her hand before he frowned again. Now, just what was she up to?

He raised his eyes, searching the surrounding area, his vision probing into the trees and underbrush. He could sense someone there, but just couldn't see anyone. He glanced back at the woman, having heard her exclamation of triumph and watched as she sat up, fidgeting with her camera before she packed it away into a backpack he hadn't seen. She rose gracefully, folding the blanket and sticking into the pack as well before she picked up the pack and stood, her gaze roaming the area. She walked forward, just as Simon heard a snap from the woods and caught a glimpse of sun reflecting off metal.

He gave a shout and charged forward, throwing himself towards the woman, arms wrapping around her as he threw them both to the ground and then covered her as best he could with his own body, his head raised just enough to glance around. He felt a tug at his jacket sleeve and then saw bursts of snow flying up just beyond them.

A startled cry had been torn from the woman and then she struggled to free herself from him, her voice sharp with fear.

"Get off me, you oaf!"

Simon finally caught her words as he glanced towards the woods, seeing that the assailant had fled, and moved away from her, sitting up and reaching out a hand to her. She turned over, slapping at his hand and pulling herself upright.

"What were you doing?" She was angry, he could tell, even though her cap had not dislodged in the fall.

"Trying to keep you safe." He responded, shocked at the vehemence of her reaction. "Someone was shooting at you."

"Not at me, boyo. More likely at you. I'm a stranger here." She rose and gathered her backpack once more. "Let's hope you didn't damage the cameras." She stood for a moment, her gaze drilling into his, her face shadowed by the sun behind her.

Simon shook his head as he rose. No, this was not Julia, his friend, Blackie's wife, but she looked almost identical to her. Now what, he thought? Lord, please help me to understand because I sure don't right now.

The woman glared at him once more before she stomped off, snow squeaking under her feet.

Simon shook his head, and then his mind turned to what had happened. He reached for his radio, knowing he would have to call it in, and also knowing he had no idea of who the woman was. He spun, seeing she had already disappeared, and sighed. Chief Waters would not like this, he decided, his eyes turning to the holes in the snow where he knew they'd find the bullets.

Chapter 2

Turning to look back towards the man she had just walked away from, Eavan Walker sighed. She had not been nice, her Gran would tell her. Not one bit. She needed to apologize, she knew. She could feel God's nudge to do just that. She stood hesitating, before she shrugged and walked away. She was sure she had seen him around town at some point, but right now, she had to get back to her studio. She had pictures she needed to take care of. She turned, heading off, her quick strides covering the ground. She didn't see the two men who emerged from the forest, one with a rifle in his hand, and stand watching her, their conversation ugly and angry.

Eavan slipped quietly into her studio, knowing the younger woman she had working for her was up front. She could hear her talking with a customer. She sighed. She wanted so much to be on her own today, didn't want to be around anyone at all, but knew she had to have Maggie out there. She herself refused to work with the customers, preferring to keep herself in the background, a shadowy figure to the studio and website she had created, entitled Reflections by Elf.

She turned as she felt a hand on her back. Her Gran, Megan Walker, stood there, a frown on her face.

"Eavan, what did you go and do this time? Your jacket's wet." Gran looked closer. "And there a hole in it. Did you go and hurt yourself, child?"

Eavan shrugged out of her jacket, seeing for the first time the tear and realizing that whoever that man had been, he had saved her. Her eyes slid closed. Now I really have to a find him, don't I, Lord, and apologize profusely? And you know how hard that will be for me, seeking out someone when I have been hiding for so many years.

"No, I didn't. Something happened today, Gran, and I don't know what to think." She shot a glance at the clock. "I'll tell you but first I have to get these pictures up and see if I caught the one Danny wanted." Her face glowed as she remembered the moment her finger had clicked on the camera and she caught the little mouse peeking out of the snow. "I think I did."

She looked around as Maggie came from the front, a troubled look on her face.

"Eavan, there's a police officer out there, wanting to speak with you." She looked over her shoulder. "He's from the county force."

Gran's hand tightened on her granddaughter's hand. "You need to talk to him."

"Not right at this moment. You know I'm on a deadline and I have exactly three hours to see if it's what Danny wants. I think it is." She brushed past the two women and into her studio, the door clicking behind her.

Simon stood at the counter in the shop, hearing the conversation, a slight smile coming over his face. The smile widened as he heard the door click shut and then the concerned voices of the two women left standing and staring at one another.

He walked away from the counter, studying the photos that hung on the wall, turning as he heard footsteps behind him.

"I'm sorry for Eavan. She will apologize for this. I'm her grandmother, Megan Walker." Her hand went out to shake Simon's even as his head tilted to pick up the lilting accent that traced her words.

"I'm Simon Gardner. I ran into your granddaughter earlier today. I just wanted to apologize to her and see if she is fine."

"By her words and actions, she is." Megan turned, her hand tucking into Simon's arm. "Now, tell me, young man. Are you in a hurry? It's almost lunch time and I have soup on the stove that I would gladly share with you."

Simon's surprise showed on his face for a moment before he shook his head and allowed Megan to lead him to the back of the studio, into the living quarters. He stood for a moment, taking in the simplicity of it, before he walked towards the kitchen, taking the bowls as Megan ladled the soup into them. She paused, her hand on one bowl, her head turning.

"I need to take this to Maggie." She reached for the tray, finding Simon's hands there before hers.

"I can do that for you. Is this ready to go out to her?"

Megan nodded, her eyes following Simon's tall, strong form as he walked back towards the front of the shop, her hand resting on her cheek. Lord, you have brought this man into our lives. He is exactly like the knights I used to weave into stories for my Eavan. Tall, strong, black curls, dark blue eyes. You knew all those years ago that she would find someone just like that.

Simon sat later, his eyes studying the albums Megan had brought to him in the living room, his thoughts on the lady who had taken the photos. He glanced at his watch. He needed to leave soon. His friends had planned a dinner among themselves and wanted him there. He sighed to himself. He felt like a fifth wheel right now, with Jacob, Blackie, and Josh all married to wonderful women, Josh and his Leah the proud parents of a beautiful little girl.

He looked up as he felt a hand on his arm. Megan stood there, her eyes on the far wall, a thoughtful look on her face before she looked down at him. She sat beside him, her hand still on his arm, hesitation in her movements.

"Megan?" She had finally convinced Simon to call her by her first name but it had taken some talking, respect for his elders drilled into his head by his parents.

"Simon, I need to ask you something and I don't want Eavan knowing I have." She looked past him towards the front of the building.

Simon's eyes were on her face as he reached to lay his hand on hers. "What is is, Megan?"

"Eavan won't like me telling you this, but she is hiding from someone. She won't tell me who, but it's been going on since she was young. I ended up raising her where her father died from a heart attack not long after her mother died from cancer. She is all that I have left in the world. I want her to be safe." She looked down. "You have come into our lives at the right time. She needs you but will fight you every step of the way.

16

That's how she is. Just trust me when I say she does really need protection. Just maybe, God willing, you can get her to open up to you."

The sudden opening of a door startled the two and Simon spun to stare towards the front, not quite sure what had happened. He heard rushing footsteps towards the front and excited voices. He rose, a frown on his face as Megan patted his arm and hurried ahead of him.

"Eavan?" Megan's voice cut through the two women's excited chatter.

Eavan almost danced across the room to her grandmother. "I got it, Gran. I got the exact picture Danny needed. I'm just waiting to hear back from him." She shoved a print into her Gran's hands. "Here. What do you think?"

Megan's eyes were on her granddaughter, seeing the excitement in her eyes, then dropped to the photo. "Oh, love. You have indeed got the very essence of his story. How on earth did you manage that?"

"God, I guess, Gran." She lifted her eyes, seeing Simon for the first time. "I got it just before this big oaf tackled me into the snow."

Simon stared at her, finally catching the hint of mischief in her eyes. "What was I supposed to do, may I ask?"

"Walk on by and take whoever it was after you with you." Eavan reached for her phone, excitement still emanating from her. "Danny? Just a moment. Let me put you on speaker. Gran and Maggie are here."

A male voice carried through the room. "Eavan, how did you ever manage to get this photo? It's just so….." His voice died away. "It's too perfect, that's so spooky. How long did you wait for that mouse?"

She began to laugh. "Not really that long. I erased the crumbs from the photo. Bribery worked."

"I don't care how much bribery you used. This is exactly what I need for the book cover. Thank you." His voice died away before he spoke again. "Thank you, Eavan. You don't know how much this means. Suzie would have loved it."

"I know, Danny. I did it for her. Your little girl loved her mice so much." She blinked back tears as Danny abruptly cut off the call.

Megan moved in to hug her granddaughter. "That pleased him, Eavan. His Suzie did love her mice. Now, come. You need to eat. I know you were out early before breakfast and didn't take time to eat, not unless you had some of those bread crumbs you laid out."

Eavan hugged her Gran as she denied doing just that. Her arm around her Gran's shoulders, she turned to the kitchen area, seeing Simon standing there, his eyes watchful.

"Gran, can I have a moment with this gentleman? I fear I owe him an apology."

Megan shook her finger at her granddaughter as she moved back towards Maggie. "Do just that, love. Come and find me when you're done. We need to pray about this attitude of yours."

"Yes, Gran. I know we do. It just keeps rearing its ugly head." She sighed as she said that before moving towards Simon and pointing back towards the kitchen. "Do you have a moment?"

"I do. We need to talk, Eavan. May I call you that?" At her nod, he continued. "My name is Simon Gardner. I'm a detective with the county force."

She nodded as she pointed to a chair at the table. "Forgive me if I eat while we talk? Gran's right. I didn't have breakfast and need something."

Simon moved towards her, pulling out a chair and gently shoving her down, before he moved to fill the soup bowl for her, placing it and the sandwich her grandmother had made for her on the table in front of her. He reached for the teapot, knowing from his conversation with Megan that Eavan loved her tea. He poured their mugs full and then finally sat across from her, finding her eyes on him.

"Eavan?"

"Simon, you didn't have to wait on me. I could have gotten my own meal."

He grinned at the disgruntled look on her face. It's going to fun getting to know her, isn't it, Lord? "I know, but I was raised a gentleman. This is what my Dad would have done and I just followed through. I'm sorry. I shouldn't have."

"No. No. It's all right, I think." Her brow wrinkled as she struggled with her emotions and her thoughts. "It's just that I haven't had a male do this for me since my Dad died."

He smiled, sadness in his eyes as he thought of his own parents, both gone now for years, disease taking them both far too young. "It's okay, Eavan. I guess I'll need to learn to ask before I do something for you."

She glared at him. "And who says there'll be another chance?"

He just shook his head at her. "I'm sure there will be." He looked down at his hands clasped around the mug. "About today. I'm sorry I tackled you so abruptly. Not that I'm sorry I kept you from getting hurt."

"Yes. About today. What was that all about anyway?" She paused, her spoon halfway to her mouth, as she watched his thoughts cross his face. "Simon?"

He shook his head. "You look so much like a friend's wife, it's spooky." He reached for his phone, then paused. "First, about today. I really am sorry I tackled you without warning. There was someone in the trees, aiming for you." He pointed to his jacket. "I have the hole in my jacket to prove it."

She paled, her spoon dropping back into her bowl, the liquid splashing outside the bowl. "Simon? Were you hurt?"

He shook his head. "We don't know if it was the man we were after or not. That's why I was out there. I was following up on a report of an armed male out there. Well, myself and other officers." He pointed to her soup. "Eat."

"You're still bossy, you know that." She finally pushed her bowl away, her appetite gone. "What is this about your friend's wife, I think you said?"

He nodded. "I need to prepare you about life in this town." He proceeded to talk, telling her about the founding families and the legacy they had left to their descendants of buildings in town, money in the bank, things that could not be sold or passed out of the families. "Blackie's Julia is one of those families." He smiled. "In fact, my three friends and myself are too. As it turns out, Jacob's Finn and Blackie's Julia are cousins. Josh's Leah is also related to Finn and Julia."

"Just a moment. You said Finn?" Her eyes were watchful.

"I did. Her full name was Finola Bronagh but everyone calls her Finn. Why?"

She paused, then sighed, knowing the Lord had brought Simon into her life, whether or not she liked it. "I was told to find a Finola Bronagh when I came here. I had a letter. Gran doesn't know about it. She also doesn't know why I had to leave where we were living."

"Will you tell me?" He watched as she tilted her mug and then went to rise. He rose, his hand on her shoulder keeping her in her chair as he moved past her, feeling the teapot and then making a fresh pot, giving her a chance to collect her thoughts.

"Simon?"

He paused as she spoke, his eyes searching hers, noting the clear green of them with the flecks of gold and brown scattered through the green, perfectly paired with her dark auburn hair.

"Eavan? What is it?"

"I think he's here. I think he's found me. I have tried so hard to hide. My studio and website don't name me as the photographer. I use an alias for that. But I know he's found me. And I'm scared." Fear shimmered in her eyes, and suddenly nothing else mattered to Simon, except keeping this lady safe and finding the one after her, no matter what it took.

Simon tried to draw out more information from her but she just shook her head, telling him she needed to organize her thoughts and find the paperwork she had somewhere, that she would track him down and give it to him, before reminding him he was to tell her about his friend's wife.

Simon pulled out his phone, flipping through to a picture of Blackie and Julia, studying it before handing his phone to Eavan.

Her hand shaking, she took it, her eyes on him before she dropped them to the picture. Her breath caught in her throat.

"That could be me, Simon. Whatever does this mean?" She looked up at him. "As far as I know, I have never been in this town in my life."

"That's what I would like to look into. If I can have your parents' names and your date of birth, I can have a friend start to research it."

She nodded, giving them to him, turning as Maggie's hand touched her shoulder. "Don't be forgetting to tell Simon you're adopted, love. Adopted as a week-old infant. Your birth certificate was sealed but I think we need to look into who your biological parents are."

Simon's hand froze as he was writing, his thoughts going to Julia and her brother, Jonathan, and the way their mother had been with them. "I have an idea, but I need to run it by someone first. Let me talk to them. In the meanwhile, I'll have my friend start his research." He held up a hand at Eavan's protest. "He will not say a word to anyone but you or I. I can guarantee you that."

Chapter 3

Simon paced the living room of his home later that night, his socked feet whispering quietly on the hardwood floors he had lovingly repaired and refurbished. He ran his hands through his hair, for what time he was sure but he knew it had been many. He was disturbed by Eavan's words and then too there was her likeness to Julia. Where did she fit into this town? He was sure it was no coincidence that she ended up here.

He paused as he heard steps on the wooden porch running across the front of his house and then a tap at the door. He approached cautiously, not expecting anyone that night. He had declined his friends' invitation to dinner, much to their disappointment and among their protests, just shaking his head at them before he walked away, leaving them staring after him.

He opened the door, surprised to see Samuel Blackwell standing here, a folder tucked under his arm. He knew Samuel well, as he was Blackie's father, but he had felt as if Samuel had at times acted in the stead of his own father.

"Samuel? Come in. What brings you out tonight?"

"I have some things to talk over with you, Simon. It's going to take a while. How full is your coffee pot?" He grinned as he followed Simon to the kitchen, knowing full well Simon drank tea but kept a coffee pot on hand for his friends.

"Sit, Samuel. Have you eaten?" Simon finally sat across from him, taking a sip of his tea, watching his friend closely. "What did you need to talk to me about?"

"This." Samuel tapped the folder he had set on the table before he slid it over, not removing his hand as Simon reached for it.

Simon lifted questioning eyes to Samuel, not quite sure why Samuel was preventing him from opening the folder.

"Simon. This is something I have prayed many hours about as has my wife.

We want you to come work with us, in a new department. We saw how hard you worked with Leah, to find her parents. We receive contact from people looking for their parents or their missing children. We want to start a new department, dedicated just to that. We want you to work it for us. We've seen the discontent and restlessness in you for the last year. Is that true?"

Simon nodded. "I have felt that way lately. Today, I decided I would resign from the force and find something to do. I just can't continue working like I am. God has been speaking to me, leading me in a different direction than He did when I moved here."

Samuel nodded. "That confirms what I have been getting in my own prayers. Pray over this decision and come to me in a week. I know you would give you answer tonight, but you need to seek this guidance from God." He nodded at the folder. "Now, Old Jack has come to me. He says he thinks Julia and Jonathan's mother may have given up a child for adoption, but he can't be sure. He says Julia's father said he finally go her mother to admit that about a week before he died and that he would going to track down this baby.”

Simon sighed as he reached for the folder, flipping it open, leafing through the pages, scanning what Samuel had already found. “This is the first one, I take it.”

Samuel nodded. “I would like to help Old Jack.” His hand went up. “I know. His name is Ben Bronagh. I’ve known for months. He confided in me.” He was puzzled by the look on Simon’s face. “Simon?”

“Just a moment.” Simon rose and padded away to his office, returning with a folder. “I think I know who the baby is. And she’s not going to accept it very well. Not at the present.” He slid his own folder over to Samuel.

Samuel gave him a startled look, before he frowned. “How do you know that already?”

“Because I spent today with the lady and her grandmother.” He nodded to the folder. “Read what I noted and then we talk. And before you asked, she agreed to a DNA sample, which you know takes time.”

Samuel finally took his eyes from his young friend and opened the folder, reading through the neat thorough notes Simon had made. He sat back, stunned at the discovery, hope welling within him as well as caution.

"Do you think it's this girl? How do you pronounce her name anyway?"

"It's pronounced Eve-een. Her parents were Irish. I've met her grandmother as well, and she's convinced that Eavan belongs in this town. Why, she refused to say."

Samuel nodded, his eyes on the photo Simon had snapped of Eavan without her being aware of it, one where she was talking with her grandmother and laughing at something she had said. "She looks so much like Julia. Please, God, let it be her."

Samuel finally stood, filled with mixed emotions, knowing he couldn't talk to his wife or even Blackie, not yet. He and Simon had work to do.

"Who is this person that's looking for Eavan, anyway, Samuel? I'm not getting good vibes about him."

"I don't either. I suggest we stall him as long as we can." He turned, compassion showing briefly in his eyes as he studied Simon. Lord, his heart's already involved, isn't it? Don't let him get hurt. "You'll need to talk to her."

"I know. I don't look forward to that." Simon had admitted to Samuel how he had met Eavan. "She'll likely call me an oaf again."

Samuel started laughing, drawing a wry smile from Simon. "If that's all she calls you, that's good, isn't it? Call me in a week and let me know what you plan. We'll see you at church in the morning."

Simon locked the door behind Samuel, already in prayer about the job offer. It was exactly what he wanted but he had to be sure. He knew without a shadow of a doubt his resignation would be on his lieutenant's desk Monday morning, regardless of whether he took Samuel's offer or not.

Eavan had turned to her grandmother after Simon had walked away late that afternoon, finding her grandmother watching her closely.

"Gran? Why did you ask him to stay for lunch? You never do that."

Megan nodded. "I know. It's as if the good Lord was telling me we needed that man in our lives, in your life. No, I'm not meddling. Just following orders." She turned and walked away, leaving Eavan standing behind her, mouth open until she closed it with a snap.

Eavan whispered a good night to her grandmother, heading for her own bedroom and quiet time with the good Lord, as her Gran called God. She had been out of line today and she knew it. Fear drove her at times. She was ready to face whoever it was and win her freedom. It had gone on long enough.

She fingered the envelope she kept tucked in her Bible, a letter directing her to this very store in Mistletoe, telling her it was rent free. She had no idea who had written the letter but she planned on finding out just that. Maybe Simon could help her, she thought, and then groaned. She had decided she needed to stand on her own two feet and figure this out on her own, and here she was planning on talking to a man she had just met.

Her hand stilled as she pictured him from that morning, sitting back in the snow, his toque in his hands, black hair in tousled curls, and she recognized what her Gran had. He was the knight in all those stories from her childhood. Gran, how did you know? She knew it was a God moment, as her Gran was wont to say.

She stood for a few minutes, the lights out, staring out her bedroom window, her eyes raised to the sky, not seeing the man standing in the shadows of a building across from her, keeping watch. It would have frightened her if she had known.

Old Jack finally turned, his head nodding. He could soon claim his rightful name. His other niece had come home to Mistletoe. He just needed help to prove it. And only one man would do. Simon would be his choice. The other three friends were too close to her, he decided. He would find Simon tomorrow and talk with him.

Chapter 4

Simon turned as he heard his name called the next morning, stopping in his walk across the church parking lot. Jacob ran towards him.

"Good morning, Simon. We missed you last night." Jacob wasn't prying, Simon knew, just concerned.

"Good morning. Where's Finn?"

"She's already in the church. Something about helping with the coffee for after church." He walked beside Simon in silence for a moment, before his hand came out and he pulled his friend to a stop. "Simon? What's going on with you?"

"What do you mean?" Simon stared at his friend, wondering where the conversation was headed.

"You're not you. Not the friend we know and love. You're restless and that I haven't seen, not since just before we all left the service. It's back."

Simon sighed, knowing he had to confide in his friend. "I am, Jacob, and could use your prayers. I'm putting in my resignation tomorrow and I really don't know what I'll do. I have had a job offer that I'm praying about."

Jacob nodded. "Finn and I wondered if you would resign. It's burning you out, Simon. You haven't been the same since you worked on Leah's case, helping her to reunite with her parents. That's what you should be doing, you know."

Simon started to laugh as he held the door for his friend. "I should, should I? I guess then I'll have to see what transpires. Now, where are you two sitting today? And don't say up front, because I will not sit with you if you do." He stopped as he felt a hand on his arm and looked down.

"Simon?" Megan stood there, looking up at him. "Would you sit with me this morning? Eavan didn't come. She's off somewhere, somewhere she won't tell me, but I know she's off to spend time in prayer and meditation. That's what she does, goes off on her own."

Simon smiled down at her. "I would be delighted, Megan, and honoured to sit with you. Now, where would you like to sit?"

"About half way to the front is good." She looked around. "What happened to the man you were talking to?"

"Jacob? Oh, he's likely gone to find his wife, Finn. I would really like to introduce you to my friends and their wives. One of the couples have a beautiful little girl who looks so much like her mother."

"Oh, I would like that. Now, this minister. I heard he's good." She settled into a pew, Simon on the end, and began to read over the program or bulletin or whatever it was called, she just could never remember.

Samuel smiled at her words. "He is very good. He also happens to be a good friend. His wife is sister to the couple I told you who have the little baby." He paused as he felt little hands patting his arm and looked down. "Heidi and Holly? What are you doing here?" He looked around for Joy, the minister's wife and saw her heading his way, a smile on her face, which turned to a frown as she saw her daughters climbing up to sit on Simon's knee.

"Heidi and Holly. Is that where you're supposed to be?" She bit back a smile as Heidi shook her head before she looked up with a smile at Simon.

Holly on the other hand nodded. "It is. Sit with Simon today."

Joy reached for her daughters, then stopped as Simon spoke to the girls, who were off his lap and headed for the pew they usually sat in.

"Simon, how did you do that?"

He shrugged and grinned. "Just asked them to do what you said and that I'd be disappointed in them if they didn't." He grinned at Joy, then introduced her to Megan, his mind wandering as he listened to their short conversation.

After church, Megan turned as she heard a voice calling for Simon to wait and searched the crowd, a frown on her face.

"Where's Eavan, Simon? I thought I heard her call you."

Simon froze, realizing what she had said. He realized that Eavan's voice had a quality just like Julia's. "It's not Eavan, Megan. It's my friend, Julia." He watched with compassion as her hand went to her mouth and tears briefly entered her eyes.

"I thought it was Eavan. She sounds like my Eavan."

Simon nodded. "I guess she does. Do you want to meet her today?"

Megan nodded. "Please, but don't tell her about Eavan. They need to meet to have that conversation."

"I won't." He reached to hug Julia as she and Blackie approached.

"We missed you last night, Simon. Blackie said you had another commitment."

"I did, Julia. It's complicated."

She began to laugh even as she shook a finger at him. "It's always complicated with you, Simon, but we understand." She looked with interest at Megan. "And who is this lovely lady, Simon?"

"Blackie.   Julia.   This is Megan Walker. She's just new to town."

"Oh, how nice.   Welcome, Mrs. Walker. This is a great time of year to come to Mistletoe. Where did you come from?"

Megan looked to Simon for help, Blackie catching her look, and then wrapping his wife in his arm.

"Give her time to adjust, Jewel, before you put her through the third degree. We need to get her used to you first." Blackie looked at Megan in apology. "Sorry about that. Julia just has to know people and how they tick. That's so different from when we first met."

Julia dug her elbow into her husband's ribs. "That you deserved this time, Blackie. Would you join us for lunch? We always head to the B&B Finn's people have for brunch on Sundays."

Simon was shaking his head. "I don't think so today, Julia. Megan needs to get home and I volunteered to escort her." He tucked Megan's hand into his elbow and escorted her away, leaving Blackie and Julia staring after them and then at one another.

"Did Simon just walk away from us?" Julia was astounded. He had never done that before.

"He did. Jewel, leave it. God knows what Simon is doing and we need to pray for him. I sense he's involved in something bad and he'll need all the help those prayers can give him."

Julia leaned against her husband, her eyes following Simon. "I fear for him sometimes, Blackie. He has such a difficult, dangerous job. Do you think he's heading for an adventure, just like we did?"

Blackie nodded as he took his wife's hand to lead her away from the church. "I think he will be. Or is already. There's something different about him today."

Simon shut the door carefully behind him before he slipped out of his shoes. He had decided not to head to the B&B after he dropped Megan off. He wanted to talk to Eavan, but she wasn't around and that worried him. Where was she, he wondered? Lord, please keep this lady safe. I fear for her and what she's about to face.

A tap at his door a couple of hours had him frowning and setting aside the book he was attempting to read, without much success. He rose to head for the front door and peeked through the door window, opening the door, surprise on his face.

"Eavan? How did you find me?"

"It wasn't hard, not really. You're well known in town, did you know that?" She gave him a smile that didn't quite reach her eyes. "Can I come in?"

"Oh, sure. Sorry about that. Here, let me have your jacket." He took it, hanging it in the closet, his eyes on the slice that went through the sleeve, knowing it was from the day before. "Can I get you anything? Tea? Water?"

"No, thank you. I'm fine." Eavan wandered through the living room, restless he could tell.

He sighed, heading for the kitchen and the kettle, making a pot of tea, placing it, mugs and cream and sugar on a tray, adding a plate of the cookies that Heidi had made for him. He smiled as he looked down at the misshaped cookies, laden with icing and sprinkles, knowing he'd eat them and not complain.

He set the tray on the coffee table, his eyes searching for Eavan, finding her standing in front of the fireplace, staring down into the fire he had lit.

"Eavan?" He approached her, not quite sure how to read her mood.

She raised her head and he saw the bleak look around her eyes before she brushed past him to pour herself a cup of tea, eyeing the cookies before she took one.

"Did one of the little girls Gran told me about make these for you?"

He grinned as he poured his own tea. "Heidi did. She is quite the character, that girl." He sat, his eyes searching her face before he nodded.

"Simon, I owe you an apology for yesterday. You scared me when you tackled me. Thank you for saving me, although I am still not sure which one of us the bullet was meant for."

"Bullets." When she stared at him, puzzled, he repeated himself. "Bullets. We found six and there were likely more."

She paled, her hand shaking enough she had to set her cup down. "Six? And there were more?" When he nodded, a grim look on his face, she sat back. "Who? Who did this, Simon?"

"That we're not sure of. But first, tell me about the photo. Yeah, the one of the mouse. How did you ever manage to catch him just as he peeked out through the snow? I swear you can see his nose and whiskers wriggling and his eyes on the crumbs."

She laughed, glad he had changed the subject for now. "I don't know. I just did. God knew I needed that particular frame and gave it to me. I've been trying over the last couple of weeks to get one just like and didn't even raise a mouse no matter how much I tried."

He nodded, knowing she was just waiting for him to ask why she had come to see him, other than to apologize.

"You're not going to ask, are you?" She sound disgruntled and frowned at him as he grinned at her.

"Nope. You'll eventually tell me. And then I'll take you back to your place."

He set his mug down as he leaned forward. "Your grandmother talked to you, didn't she? Told you about Julia?"

She nodded. "She did. It really threw her, seeing Julia. She said it was almost like looking at me and she said her voice was a lot like mine. How can that be? We don't even know if we are related."

"No, we don't. We can run DNA testing but that will take months. I did ask my friend to start that investigation we talked about. Stay right there. I'll be right back." He rose and headed for his office, grabbing the file Samuel had give him. He returned to the living room, this time to sit beside her, his hand on the closed file. "He has found preliminary information, Eavan. This contains it."

She looked at the folder, studying his strong hand at the same time, wanting to know what it would be like to have him hold hers when she was scared. "What does it say?" When he didn't answer, she looked up at him. "Simon?"

He shook his head, dispelling a vision of them together for the rest of their lives. That wasn't likely to happen, he thought.

"Somehow, Samuel pulled strings and found your original birth certificate. I haven't looked at the folder yet. It was late last night when he came over and with church today and other things, I just let it sit." He looked down at it. "So, this is all new to me too." He handed it to her.

She opened it, seeing photos of herself from her driver's license and other photos. "How did he find these? I didn't think I had had that many taken of me. I hide in the background."

Simon suddenly stared at her. "You were the photographer, weren't you?"

"When?" She was puzzled, not quite sure what he meant.

"At Josh and Leah's baby dedication. That's why you seem familiar."

She sighed. "I was. I didn't realize you knew them. I was in and out and tried to keep my identity as hidden as much as I can. If I remember rightly, her mother hired me through my website, so I never met them in person."

"No, I don't think you did. She mentioned afterwards that she hadn't had a chance to talk with you. You kept a hat on at all times."

"I did when I was doing sessions like that. It helped to hide my face, but it also helped to cut lighting so I could see better." She turned back to the folder, her hand stilling as she reached for a birth certificate, her eyes going to his.

"Do you want me to look at it first?"

She nodded. "Please." Her hands shook as she handed him the paper.

He watched her face for a few minutes before he dropped his eyes. He drew his breath in sharply, and his eyes rose to her, seeing the fear and apprehension and yes hope in hers.

"Simon? What does it say?"

Simon reached to wrap an arm around her, surprising her. "It's what we thought, Eavan. You are Julia and Jonathan's sister. You have a sister and a brother."

"I do? You didn't say anything about a brother."

"Yes, a brother. Oh and an uncle too."

"An uncle? This is getting bizarre. Who would he be?"

"Do you know Old Jack?"

"Old Jack? Sure. Everyone in town knows him." She waited for him to continue, her eyes on the birth certificate. At his silence, she looked up. "He's my uncle?"

Simon nodded. "His name is not Old Jack. That's just a name he chose to use for now. His name is Ben Bronagh. He's your father's brother. There is a long history with your parents that we'll need to discuss. But that's for another night. This is enough of a surprise for you."

She nodded, tears on her cheeks as she swiped at them. "This changes my whole history, you know. I know Gran will still be my Gran, but this will change that. I always knew I was adopted but never really thought about who and why." She looked up at him. "You know why, don't you?"

Simon sighed as he drew her closer to him, his cheek going down on her hair. "I have some idea. Samuel, my friend and actually Julia's father-in-law, runs an investigative firm. He has asked me to come on board and head up a new department. Yours would be the first investigation I undertake."

"Mine? You? But you're a police officer."

He shook his head. "I spoke with my lieutenant today and resigned. With accrued sick time and vacation time, I have enough time so I don't have to report back until I quit. I have to go in for a while tomorrow just to do the paperwork and finish off what I need to do. Then I am full time on this."

"But you can't. Who will pay you?"

"Samuel will. Besides, I don't need to work. With the founding fathers setting it up for their descendants, I have property and a bank account that came down through my father. You see, the Bronaghs and my friends and I are all descendants of the original five founding fathers."

"You are? How does that work?" She shook her head even as she stood, gathering their mugs and picking up the tray, heading for his kitchen. "That I can't understand tonight. My brain has had enough." She paused before she turned back to him. "How do I tell Gran?"

"She already knows, love. She already knows. She met Julia, remember?" He didn't realize an endearment had slipped into his words, but Eavan did and wondered at it.

"I think I need to go now, Simon. I think I'll be awake all night just in prayer."

"You and me both, love. Come on. Let's get you back to your Gran."

Chapter 5

Samuel stood late the next morning in Eavan's studio, looking around at the framed prints. Simon was right, he thought. She has such talent. He thought of the photos Josh and Leah had of baby Rebecca and smiled. Yes, Eavan definitely had talent and it was a shame she had to hide.

He turned as he heard a voice behind him, startled for a moment at the similarity to Julia's. He eyed the young woman in front of him, seeing the similarities that Simon had mentioned. It was spooky, he thought. Lord, help me to help this young woman. I can tell already she has Simon's heart. He has fallen hard and fast, but won't admit it, not yet any way. It was the same with Levi and Julia. He knew right away.

"Can I help you?" Eavan studied the man staring at her, puzzled at his look.

"I'm sorry. I didn't mean to stare." Samuel walked up to the counter, setting down the package that he carried. "I'm

Samuel Blackwell. Simon is a good friend of my son, Levi. Or you would have heard of him as Blackie."

"Blackie. That would be Julia's Blackie, if I understand correctly." At his nod, she studied him more openly. "And what can I be doing for you today?"

Samuel smiled at her choice of words, knowing it was likely how her grandmother would have worded the question.

"I understand from Simon that he talked to you yesterday?" He waited until she gave a reluctant nod. "I'm not prying into that conversation, trust me. That was between you and Simon and will remain that way unless either one of you talk to me. That's how I work. I trust the men and women I employ to do their task and come to me if needed. You can't do the kind of work we do if the operatives are micro-managed."

He paused, his heart lifting up in a prayer for the words he needed to say.

She poked at the parcel with one long finger. "And what would be in that?"

He laughed openly at that. She was like Julia, he thought, not wanting to see what was there but still wanting to know. "This is from my wife and I. Julia is a beloved member of our family. Besides Levi, we have two daughters, and we consider Julia a daughter." He nodded at that package. "In that, you'll find photos, letters, what have you from my wife and I, from our girls, from Levi, and more importantly from Julia, from Jonathan." He held up a hand at her protest.

"But they don't know me. Simon promised he wouldn't tell anyone." Tears clouded her vision and she fidgeted with a pen on the counter until a strong hand laid on top of hers stopped her movement.

"We have suspected for a year or so that there was another baby. Ben has confirmed that your father knew and had planned to look for the baby before he was killed." Her eyes shot to his at that. "Yes, your father was killed. I won't go into those facts yet but we will need to talk, either you and I or Simon and you."

She nodded. "Then how did you get all this so soon?" She was genuinely puzzled by that.

"Over the past year, we have all taken photos of ourselves, of places we love, or events we have been involved in. We have all taken time to write letters to the baby sister none of us know. That is, until now. Welcome to the family, Eavan. You will never know the relief I felt when Simon came to me and asked for my help in finding out about you." He held up a hand again as she went to protest. "He didn't go through official police investigative channels to do this. He chose to keep it between himself and me until you give permission for us to share with the family." He nodded towards Megan, who stood in the doorway behind her.

Eavan turned, seeing her Gran there, and reaching out a hand. Megan wrapped her granddaughter in her arms as she wept, heartbreaking sobs wracking her body. Samuel stood, uncertain as to what he should do. He finally nodded to Megan and turned and walked away, standing outside the building, his face raised to the sky, his eyes closed as he prayed for the two women he had just left inside.

Simon stood for a moment, puzzled before he walked towards Samuel, only to have Samuel turn and walk away from him, not having seen him. Simon hesitated, then walked through the door, hearing voices from the back of the building, and heading that way.

Megan turned to him, a helpless look on her face, as she was unable to comfort Eavan. Simon nodded, his jacket tossed to one side, as he sat and gathered Eavan into his arms, turned her face into his shoulder, his clasp as tight as she needed.

Eavan finally relaxed, her sobs easing, her hand clutching Simon's tightly. She didn't see her Gran reach in with a warm damp cloth but felt the softness on her face. She finally tilted her head back to look up at Simon, finding his deep blue eyes on her.

"Simon?"

"Yes, love? You all done with the waterworks?" He gave a small grin at her frown. "What happened?"

"Your friend was here." She pointed towards the front of the building. "He left a package there. Letters from the family, photos, and I don't remember what all. He said they've been preparing them over the last year."

"They have, love. That they have. They have wanted to meet you for so long now. Jonathan, your brother, knew something was wrong when he was a child, when your biological mother disappeared for a few months. He could never get an answer as to where she was. When your father was killed, he dropped it, afraid he would be next if he kept asking questions. Julia, she never said much, but one time she did say she really wanted a sister but was glad she didn't. She wouldn't have wanted her to go through the abuse she suffered at the hands of her stepfather and her mother."

"Her mother? Why? What did she do?" Eavan sat back further, her eyes not leaving his face.

"She was abusive. She was part of the plot to have your biological father killed, thinking she would get his lands and money. The way the charter works in this town is that it does to the children, not the spouses. If there are no children, then it goes into a trust for the remaining families."

"Oh, that's so horrible. How could she?" Eavan's head went back down on Simon's shoulder, not realizing that's what she had done. "And that means she's my mother too. Gran?" Eavan sat up, struggling to free herself from Simon's arms, searching for her Grandmother, who had been her steady rock all of her life.

Megan was there, sitting on beside Eavan, her arms coming around the younger couple as she prayed for them, her words inaudible as her heart broke for her beloved granddaughter.

Simon kept his eyes on Eavan's face, seeing the fear, no, terror, he thought, and knew he needed to get her to open up to him and soon. He could feel something closing in on her and wanted to protect her as much as he could. He hadn't acknowledged it yet, not really, but he wanted to get to know her better. He just knew God had brought her to him for a reason.

Eavan finally stood, heading for her bedroom. Simon stood as well, his eyes following her before he looked down at Megan, whose hand was laid on his arm.

"Let her have a few moments, Simon. She needs that." Megan headed for the front of the shop, returned with Samuel's package, and then going back to the front as the door chimed for a customer.

Simon stirred his mug of tea absentmindedly, his thoughts on the lady he had just been holding to comfort. He sighed. Lord, I have no idea what I'm in for, but You do. Guide each step. Bring comfort to my lady love.

He turned as he heard a small sound behind him. Eavan stood there, almost shamefacedly facing him. He walked towards her, his finger going under her chin to tilt her face to him.

"Look at me, love." When she did, his heart broke at the devastation he saw resting in her eyes. "It's not your fault. None of this is. Your biological mother and her second husband made choices that were wrong and they alone have to answer for them." He pointed to the package. "Now, this. I understand Samuel has been around."

"How did you know? Did you talk to him?" Her voice was barely above a whisper.

He shook his head. "No, I saw him leaving. We need to talk, you and I. I have news other than what we've talked about."

Fear suddenly coursed through her. How did he find out, she wondered? How did he know what she was running from?

He tilted his head to watch the emotions flickering across her face and made a decision.

"Can your Gran run the shop for a couple of hours?"

She nodded. "Why?"

"Because you and I are going for a drive. Leave the package. You're not ready for that yet. I need to talk to you and I would rather your Gran didn't hear, not yet anyway."

She stood for a moment, rebellion rising within her, her eyes on his. He didn't force her, letting her make her choice. She sighed, knowing that she would go with him. She turned, and his hand came to stop her.

"Eavan, love, we don't have to. We can talk here, if you would rather. I won't force you to do anything you don't want to or are not comfortable doing."

She turned as he spoke, searching his face, seeing he spoke from his heart. His heart was in his eyes, without him knowing she could see it. She finally nodded and moved to hug him.

Simon stood for a moment, before he reached for his jacket and shrugged into it, reaching for his keys. He headed to the front, watching as Megan dealt with the customers who had come in, her voice low and pleasant. He waved as she turned, holding up his keys and pointing towards the living quarters. She nodded, then her attention was back on her customer.

Eavan watched as Simon drove away from Mistletoe, not quite sure where he was heading, but feeling safe for the first time in years. Whoever it was that had haunted her seemed so far away today, but she knew that person was still out there, somewhere.

"Eavan?" He glanced at her, not quite sure where her thoughts were.

"Simon? Where are we heading?"

"To Merryville. There's a spot there I think you'll like. I'll bring you back one day and you can bring your camera. Right now, it's the most peaceful spot I can think of. Mistletoe is getting busy, leading up to the tree lighting this Saturday."

"Is that why? I wondered." She watched carefully as he pulled into a parking lot and then came around to open her door, his hand out to help her from the car.

He didn't let go on her hand as he walked them towards a gazebo set in the middle of a park. He searched the area, knowing an officer was patrolling there, having been requested. He sat Eavan down on the bench and then sat beside her, leaning forward with his arms on his thighs, his eyes on the ground.

"Simon?" Eavan's soft voice reached him but he didn't turn to look at her. He felt her hand on his back and finally straightened up, his eyes on her face. Lord, I need words and I don't have them.

"Eavan. I need to talk to you and suddenly I just don't have the words." He searched his mind but couldn't find them. "I really do need to talk to you."

She began to laugh, drawing a frown from him. "That was just so definite, Simon. What is it about? Start there."

He sighed, his arm suddenly going around her and drawing her close to him, surprise on her face at his movement.

"Who's chasing you, love? I know someone is."

"And how would you know that?" She was startled at how easily he went straight to the heart of her troubles.

"I was an MP in the forces, a police officer now. I've learned to read people. You're running. Run to me, please, Eavan. Let me help you."

She finally nodded, her eyes searching his before she turned to stare across the park, a frown now in place.

"I'm still not sure how you knew, Simon, but you're right. For the last ten years, someone has been tracking me. That's why the website and the studio don't mention me by name. I use an alias. But somehow someone has found out the alias and is taunting me. I have no idea why. His taunts are now turning to threats. I haven't shared them with anyone. I can't tell Gran. I haven't felt comfortable in going to the police. I did when it first started and it was brushed aside and I was made to feel that I was making it all up."

"You're not. You never have been. Walk be back through what has happened, starting at the very beginning." He pulled out a notebook and pen.

She missed his arm around her when he moved and wondered at that. "Okay. Let's see. This is hard, Simon." A distressed look covered her face but she refused to cry. She had wept enough over the situation, she refused to weep any more. Lord, is Simon the one? Is he the one who will stop this maniac and his threats? I can handle the threats directed at me, but now that he's going after Gran, I need to stop him.

"I know it is, love, but we need to go back to the very beginning. I know you don't want your grandmother to hear, that's a given."

She nodded, then began to speak, taking him back to the beginning of her troubles, back to when she was just seventeen and starting out with her photography. She paused intermittently to gather her thoughts, to go back over something with him, willing to answer any question he posed, and he didn't ask many, just let her talk.

Simon read back through his notes, a chill running through him. Whoever this was, he or she was getting more and more vicious and threatening more and more violence. How Eavan had survived this long, he had no idea.

He looked across the park, gathering his thoughts, a frown coming to his face as he saw movement. He rose abruptly, pulling Eavan to her feet and placing himself between what he had seen and her.

"Simon?" Her voice was questioning, but he could see the fright coming into her face.

"Someone is out there, love. An officer is responding. I made sure to have someone here on the perimeter. Let's go somewhere we can get warmed up."

He ushered into a restaurant and to a booth at the back, to the seat facing the front of the building, and sliding in beside her.

She looked at him and then pointed to the seat across from them. "You could sit there, you know. It's empty."

Simon laughed. "I could, but I would rather sit here. They have to get through me to get to you, this way."

She stared at him, disbelief and then fear on her face. He hated that. He wanted this all over for her. He gave their orders and she wondered that he ordered a coffee, when they both drank tea. Her eyes on him, she didn't see the man approaching their booth, who stopped, a hand going to his mouth for a moment as he worked to control his emotions.

Simon looked up and nodded, drawing Eavan's eyes to the man. She watched as he finally slid into the booth across from them, his eyes on her, his mouth working as he tried to speak and was unable to.

"Eavan. I'm sorry to surprise you like this, but I needed help, and this man is the one, the best one, who can." He turned to

the man, who nodded, giving his agreement
to the unasked question.

"Eavan. This is Old Jack as he is
known in town. But he is your Uncle Ben,
your biological father's brother. He has
information that we need and he has agreed
to help."

Chapter 6

*S*hocked beyond what she had ever been, Eavan stared at the older man, not quite sure how to respond. She watched as the man blinked back tears, compassion flowing through her.

"Hi. I'm not quite sure what to say." Eavan looked at Ben and then up at Simon, who sat quietly beside her, a small smile on his face, acceptance on his face. "I never knew. I'm sorry."

"That's okay, girl." Ben's voice was rough with emotion. "I know it's not your fault. It's your biological mother's fault, that's where the fault lies. But you're here now." He paused, reaching for his handkerchief to wipe at his eyes, then reached for the coffee Simon had ordered him.

He finally looked back at Eavan, seeing the tears sparkling on her lashes. "It's like this, girl. Your daddy told me that he had found out he had another daughter, that your mother had given up for adoption as soon as she was born. She had left town before he ever knew that you were on the way. He had finally confronted her, gotten her confirmation, and told me he was heading off to find out about you. He was killed one week later."

She nodded. "Simon mentioned that. But I don't see what that has to do with what I'm going through now."

Ben lifted a hand, silencing her. "I'm coming to that. Hold your horses, girl." He shot a quick look at Simon who was trying to hold back his laughter. "Silence, boy." He shook his head.

"But I'm afraid I still don't understand. How did he not know?"

"That I am afraid we'll never know. I've been and talked to her in prison. She just sits there, stone faced, not saying a word."

"She's in prison?"

Simon spoke up. "She is. She was charged with abuse and murder as well as attempted murder. She tried to kill Julia."

Eavan's breath sucked in so quickly she choked. When she could breathe again, she stared between the two men, seeng confirmation and compassion their faces

Her eyes traced to the front window and she froze. "Simon. He's out there. In that black truck."

Simon followed her line of sight. "You're sure?" When she nodded, he rose, grabbing his jacket. "Ben, stay with her."

Simon was out the door and approaching the truck before she could stop him. She glared at Ben, motioning him to follow Simon.

"Not happening, girl. He left me to watch you. He's a big boy. He can take care of himself."

"Not with the one who is after me. I'm afraid he'll get hurt." She looked up in alarm as she heard squealing tires and shouts from the street, on her feet and running for the door before Ben could stop her. He sighed, grabbed her jacket, even as he dropped money on the table, and ran after her. *I'm getting too old for this, Lord.*

Would you be so kind as to settle all these young ones down?

He searched for Eavan, finding her on her knees beside Simon's still body, her hands assessing him even as she spoke with the officer kneeling across from her.

"Here, girl. On your feet. The paramedics are here. Let them work." Ben drew her to her feet, shoving her arms into her jacket, and then standing with an arm around her. "We'll follow them to the hospital."

He turned as he heard his name called and saw Simon's commanding officer approaching him.

"Old Jack? What happened? Someone said Simon was run down."

Ben nodded grimly. "First, let me correct you. The name's really Ben Bronagh. I've been living undercover for a while now." He nodded towards where they were still assessing Simon, pulling out the neck brace and the backboard. "He was run down. He's helping this young lady and he came out to talk to someone she recognized as being after her."

The man stared at Eavan for a moment. "That's not Blackie's Julia, now is it?"

Ben shook his head. "We've just found out it's her younger sister. That's not for common knowledge yet." He tightened his hold on Eavan as she went to move towards the ambulance. "They won't let you ride with him, girl."

The officer with them shook his head. "Let her go. I'll clear it for her. If what you say is true, then we'll need to provide protection for them while they're here." He was as good as his word. "Now, where is Simon's vehicle? I have his keys and will have it taken to his home. He won't be driving it, not today."

Eavan was scrambling into the back of the ambulance before anyone could say a word, tucking herself back into a corner out of the way, her eyes on Simon. She hated that he had been hurt because of her. Or was it? She really wasn't sure. Not any more.

She followed the stretcher as it was wheeled into the Emergency Department, coming to a stop near the head of it, refusing to move when she was asked to leave the room.

Ben finally found her and arm around her, pulled her from the room and out to a chair, where he gently pushed her down, sitting beside her.

"Let them work on him, girl. They'll come get you." He nodded towards the rooms. "What did you tell them to make them let you stay?"

She shook her head, her eyes not leaving the hallway. "I didn't say anything. I think they thought I was his girlfriend or something."

"That would be about right." He looked around, knowing that Julia and Blackie were on their way. The other two couples had been away for the day together and weren't expected back until later. He hesitated as he saw the man approaching him.

Why now, Lord? I have to have time to prepare him and now I don't.

"Uncle Ben? I heard Simon was brought in. What happened?" Jonathan Bronagh stood there, worry on his face.

"He was, son. That he was. We're waiting on word now."

Jonathan looked around, not recognizing anyone else. "We? Who's we?" He looked up, stepping back as Eavan approached them. "Uncle Ben? Who is this?"

Eavan stared at the younger man, seeing traces of her own features in him. Ben's arm came around her and he pointed them towards a seating area away from the others.

"Jonathan, this is not how I wanted to do this. Simon was to speak with you." Ben looked down at his clasped hands. "You know what your father had discovered and didn't get a chance to investigate." He nodded towards Eavan. "This is the baby that your mother gave away. This is your youngest sister, Eavan Walker. She was adopted when a week old and just in the last few days has found out who her biological parents are."

Jonathan sat back, stunned at the revelation. He turned to Eavan, seeing her sitting there composed. As he went to speak to hear, she rose and walked away, towards the nurse heading her way and then following her from the waiting room.

"Uncle Ben? How?"

"I don't know all that happened. Simon knows more. Someone is after her, though. We think that it is why he was run down today."

Jonathan shook his head, reaching for the young woman who sank down beside him. Ben reached over to drop a kiss on Jonathan's wife, Bev's, cheek.

A commotion at the door raised their hands. Jonathan groaned.

"Leave it to Julia to make an entrance." He rose and headed towards her, his steps slowing and finally stopping as he watched Julia head for the desk, her own footsteps stopping as she stared at the woman walking towards her. Julia's eyes followed her as the woman approached Ben.

"Uncle Ben? They've said Simon can go home in about an hour. Will you take us home? I heard the officer say he would have his car driven to his place."

Ben reached to hug Eavan, even as he agreed to drive her and Simon home.

"Where's he going to go? They won't let him be on his own."

"I know. I called Gran. He'll be welcome to use our spare room for the next few days, if you can grab him some clothes." She stopped, suddenly feeling eyes on her, and turned, coming face to face with a young woman who almost looked like her twin.

They stared at each other, before Julia looked past Eavan to Ben.

"Uncle Ben? Who is this?"

Ben moved towards Julia, even as Blackie wrapped an arm around his wife. Eavan's heart sank, realizing who this and suddenly afraid, wishing with all her heart she had Simon beside her, to buffer this meeting.

"Julia. Keep your voice down, please." Ben stared at his niece until she looked shamefaced and nodded. "There is an explanation due to both you and Jonathan, but now is not the time or place. Suffice it to say, the baby your father wanted to look for is Eaven. This is your baby sister, the sister you always wanted."

Julia's face revealed her shock and puzzlement even as she felt Blackie's arm tighten around her.

"Let it go for now, Jewel. Simon or Ben will explain it all. Right now, Simon's the important one." Blackie's soft words settled Julia's emotions somewhat and she looked back at the young woman, who stood, apprehension on her face, before she turned and walked back towards the exam rooms.

Jonathan reached for his sister, drawing her into a hug, knowing just how this had affected her.

"Are you okay?" He finally asked, leaning back to look down at her.

"I think so. I didn't expect this." She turned with a frown. "But I don't understand how she's back there. Simon didn't say he was dating anyone."

Ben gave a wry grin as he turned her back to face him, moving Jonathan aside to do so. "For now, he is. We need to keep this as low key as we can and right now we're not. I would suggest you and Blackie and Jonathan and Bev head out. I'll call you tomorrow. Take tonight to pray, Julia, about this and your attitude." He gave her a stern look until she nodded.

Blackie waved as he headed off with Julia, her hand tight in his. This was not what either had expected when they showed up here.

"Julia?" Blackie was concerned about her.

"It will take time to sink in, love. I just never expected to have a sister."

"I know. Now, let's do what Ben said. I think we'll need to let him or Simon talk to Jacob and Josh. It's their place, not ours."

Simon settled down carefully onto the bed, nodding as Ben lifted his feet to the bed and then pulled the covers over him. Simon was sore and had a wicked headache, but all things considered, he thought, I came off fortunate.

"Eavan's okay?" He was concerned as he watched Ben fold his shirt and jeans and lay them handy for the morning.

"She is, son, but she's scared. She's ready to do something she shouldn't, I think."

Ben stood for a moment, then sank down into a chair. "I know you're hurting, but we need to talk, son. Julia and Jonathan both showed up at the hospital, and met Eavan. Not at all how it should have been."

Simon sighed. "I know. I wanted to prepare them. Now we'll need to warn Blackie to watch Julia. They look enough alike that they may take Julia by mistake."

"That's what I'm thinking." Ben suddenly grinned, causing Simon to frown at him. "Did you know Eavan let on that she was your girlfriend at the hospital? The nurses assumed that she was, she just wouldn't leave you."

"She didn't, did she?" He stared at Ben for a moment, dumbfounded. "And Julia walked in on that, didn't she?"

Ben nodded, knowing what Simon was thinking. "Blackie will talk to her. All she knows is that she suddenly has a sister and nothing more." He looked up as a tap came to the door and then rose and opened it.

Eavan stood there, hesitating, a tray in her hands that she shoved at Ben. "Gran thought Simon might want some soup or tea or something. She thought he'd need something on his tummy, as she put it, when he took his pain medications." She waited until Ben had taken the tray she kept shoving at him before she turned and fled. He watched as the door to her studio closed quietly behind her, shaking his head as he did so.

"Ben?"

Ben turned, coming over to set the tray down. "You'll have to eat something of that, you know, son."

Simon nodded, hardly able to keep his eyes open. "Let me have a moment, please. Watch Eavan. I have no idea what she'll try. I don't know her well enough…" His words died off as he slept.

Ben stood for a moment, watching him sleep, before he picked up the tray and headed for the kitchen. He cleaned up the dishes and then turned, startled to see Eavan standing there, a look on her face he couldn't read.

"Uncle Ben? Talk to me. Tell me what happened. Why I was given up."

Ben sighed to himself. He was exhausted but he knew his day was far from over. This young lady needed answers, some he had, more that he didn't have.

Chapter 7

*S*imon stared at Megan late the next morning, not quite sure he had heard her right

"She did what? She went where?"

"What I said, young man. Now, sit. Here's some soup for you. You're not to have anything solid for another day. That's what the doctor told Eavan."

He sat, mutiny in his heart, before he prayed, asking for forgiveness and a right heart.

"But where would she go?"

Megan shrugged. "I have no idea. She's an adult. She does not answer to me about her comings and her goings." She held up a hand to stop his protest. "She has done this all her life. When she needs to think, she grabs a camera and goes for a walk. Some of her best photos have come from those walks." She sat beside him, her hand just beginning to show the changes arthritis was wreaking in it on his, keeping his on the table. "You need to understand, Simon. She can't be caged. It would kill her. She was like that even as a toddler. Always up for an adventure. I can't begin to tell you the times her parents and I would search for her, to find her walking towards us, a flower or a leaf or a pretty rock in her hand. If you are going to be part of her life, let her have her freedom and solitude. It makes her who she is."

He nodded. "I get that. I'm just worried about her safety, that's all."

"We all are. Ben and I had a good talk this morning before he headed out. I know what she's facing here." She paused, her eyes on their hands as she squeezed his, a prayer in her heart for his understanding. She had seen the looks they were sending one another, each hoping the other wasn't watching them at the time. She could see them falling in love with each other more and more each day. Her prayer had become a prayer for peace for them, for them to realize how much they loved one another.

"But she's facing so much right now." Simon gave a small smile as Megan shook her head at him.

"I know what she's facing here in town, or some of it. I am also well aware of what she's been facing over the years. Whatever she received, I received." She rose, heading for her bedroom, returning with a large manilla envelope that she handed him. "This is for you. Look through it. Eavan has no idea I have these. Please, Simon. Keep her safe. For my sake, and for yours."

"I will do my best, Megan. Trust me on that." He looked down at the enveloped, then reached to open it, her hand stopping him as he did so. "Don't open it here. Take it to the room you used, or wait until you go home today. Eavan doesn't need to see this."

He nodded once more, rising to put it with his bag that Ben had brought in for him. He turned as he heard Eavan's happy laughter and headed her way, desperate to see her. He smiled to himself as he thought of her pretending to be his girlfriend the day before. Suddenly, that was a wish he wanted to come true, that she really was his.

Eavan looked up as Simon appeared at the counter in the studio, her face alight with excitement.

"I did it again, Simon. I got another photo I've been trying to get for months." She danced towards him, enveloping him into a hug and holding on just a little bit longer. "How are you feeling today?"

"Sore. The headache better. Ticked off with a young lady." He tried to frown but was unsuccessful. "What photo is that?"

She caught his hand and drew him to the counter. "Here. See this? Someone wanted a close up of a certain type of snowflake. It's so hard to photograph a snowflake, but I did it."

He stared down at the photo, seeing her talent afresh. "You really did, didn't you?"

She nodded. "I did. Now, I just have to finish it off and send it to the client." She turned, her eyes on him. "We need to talk, Simon. I met both Jonathan and Julia last night. Neither one knew about me. I don't like that."

He held up his hands and then pointed at the photo. "Finish with that and then we'll talk. I promise. We didn't have time to talk to either one of them, remember?" His words at the end had a bite to them that drew her back, and then she nodded.

"I realize that, but that doesn't mean I still have to like it. I don't."

She turned and walked away from him, her mind already on her photo and what she needed to do it. Not much, she decided. She sighed as she sank down in front of the large monitor on her desk. Yes, Lord, I get it. I will apologize once again to Simon. I just don't know what I let him get to me like I do.

She finished her work, sent off the proof the client, and then sat back, a sense of foreboding once again coming over her. Lord, are you preparing me for something? I feel that You are, something dangerous and life threatening. I need Your strength and courage from You today.

Simon turned from the front window of her studio where he had stood, watchful for anyone or anything he felt was out of place. So far, he hadn't seen anything, but he knew someone was watching her. He had found evidence of that, as had Chief Waters. He had talked to the Chief earlier and brought him up to date on what was happening.

The Chief had listened to him, given some advice, and then asked what his plans were, since he was quitting the county force. He could use him on the town force, he hinted. Simon had just laughed, told him he was praying over a job offer, and that he wasn't leaving town. Not at all.

Eavan hesitated, then reached out a hand for Simon. Maggie had locked up and gone home, her day done, so it was just the two of them right then. She could heard her Gran in the kitchen, singing an old beloved hymn in her sweet alto, preparing their evening meal.

Simon drew Eavan into a hug, knowing both of them needed it. Eavan started and then wrapped her own arms around Simon, feeling safe and secure again.

She finally moved back from him, her eyes going everywhere but to him.

"You wanted to talk, Simon?" She finally perched on the stool behind the counter, her hands idly tidying already neat piles of cards and samples of photos.

He reached for her hands, his warm and strong on hers, as he stilled her movements. She finally looked up at him, seeing his heart in his eyes and knowing he didn't realize it was there. She smiled and reached to kiss his cheek.

Simon froze for a moment, then nodded. "We do." He pulled up another stool, his hands going back to hold hers when he was settled. "Ben told me what happened at the hospital. He says you met both Jonathan and Julia."

"I did. I wasn't prepared for that, Simon. I was told worried about you to really take in that anyone else was there." She sighed. "I don't think I made a very good impression, taking over her Uncle Ben like I did, without her knowing. I was with Uncle Ben when he talked to Jonathan and his wife."

"His wife? Jonathan's married? He never said, but then he hasn't been around much for the last year."

"He is. Her name is Bev." Her eyes fell to their hands, as she tried to organize her thoughts. "I don't think Julia was very happy to find out about me."

Simon reached to hug her. "Oh, I think she was. She has wanted a sister so badly for so long. Jonathan left as soon as he could, I can't remember all the circumstances why. But Julia will be happy." He sighed, pulling out his phone. "I hate this. Every time I get into a really good conversation, my phone rings."

"That's why I don't carry one."

"You don't? From now on, you do. Give me yours later and I'll program in some numbers for you."

She nodded, then looked back at the desk, not quite sure how to start. "I don't know where to begin, Simon. I think I've shuttered it away, not wanting to face it."

He waited, letting her gather her thoughts, his experience being that any victim needed this time, a time to reflect and regroup.

"You said it started when you were 17? What triggered that, do you know?"

She shrugged. "I have no idea. I remember whoever it was said something about my photo. Did I pick up something I shouldn't have?"

Simon nodded. "You may have and not even known it. Do you have a copy of it?"

She spun on her stool, grabbed his hand and almost ran for her studio. She hunted through a filing cabinet, pulling out a folder, and opening it on the table in the room. "This is it. I have the negatives. I can enlarge it if I have to."

"We can scan it as well to your computer. The quality may not be the best but we can try. I can also take it to our lab or Chief Waters can do that." He studied the photo. "Do you have a magnifying glass?"

She hunted for one, handing it to him. She watched as he scanned the photo once more, stopping at a particular section.

"There, Eaven. There. That's what he's been after all these years. You did pick up on something without knowing it."

She stared at him, horrified at the thought. "What did I do?"

"Here. We'll need to enlarge it, but I think there's someone or something lying on the ground and someone standing in the shadows."

With trembling hand, she reached for the photo and then turned, determination in her stride, to her scanner, sending the photo to her computer. She sat, bringing up her photo program, and hunting for the area Simon had pointed to, enlarging it.

"You're right. I never noticed this before. I was too focused on the overall picture." She printed copies on the enlargement, pulling them off the printer and handing them to Simon. "Now what? Is this what all this has been about?"

Simon shrugged. "I think it's part of it. But I also think someone has watched you since you were a baby, trying to figure out how to get the property that comes to you."

"What property? I have no interest in anything other than what I have." She was shocked, having forgotten what Simon had told her.

"You're part of this town, love, whether you admit it or not. And as such, as a descendant of the founding families, you have property and money coming to you."

"I don't want it."

Simon grinned at her. "I hate to tell you this, but this building? It's actually yours. Ben checked into it today for me."

She stared at him, then went to the door of the office to stare around the studio. "This is mine?" She spun. "So I can do what I want, remodel it how I want to?"

He nodded, grinning at the excitement he could see coming from her, reaching to hug her tightly as she sputtered out plans. He leaned back to look down at her, seeing her heart in her eyes, and knowing he had found his lady, his love, that God had provided for him after all, after all those years.

"I hear tell you let on you were my girlfriend yesterday." He grinned as she struggled to get away from him, holding on tighter. "I just want you to know that is what I want too. I want you to be my girlfriend for now. And then we'll see from there. Will you?"

She stared up at him, realizing that as tall as she was for a lady, he was still a lot taller and that she fit just right into his arms. "I guess….I guess." Her words sputtered to a stop as his body shook with his suppressed laughter. "Stop laughing at me, Simon. I can't think with you this close."

"Well, then I guess I'll have to stay this close. I like it when you can't think." He grinned at her as she shook her head.

"What I was trying to say is that yes, I would be delighted to be your girlfriend, unless you don't let me go. Then I'll start calling you an oaf again."

He laughed at her words. "I could get used to that term of endearment. Now, Gran has supper ready, I can tell. Let's go eat. Then I need to head off."

Chapter 8

Simon looked up from his office in Samuel's building as Samuel tapped at his door and then entered, closing the door behind him before he sank into one of the chairs in front of Simon's desk. It had been four days since Simon had been run down and the police were no closer to finding his assailant that they had been that day.

"Simon? I ran that photo you provided. You will not like the name I came up with."

Simon sat back, his pen rolling in his fingers. "Somehow I didn't think I would."

"Your girlfriend has been fortunate so far that she's stayed out of his hands. Not knowing has been to her advantage. Now that she knows he's in that photo, it will be worse for her."

Simon nodded. "Just who are we talking about?"

When Samuel said the name, Simon paled, his pen dropping to his desktop. "I thought he was dead."

"He is, but his son has taken on his holdings and is even more vicious and dangerous than his father. Law enforcement all over are looking for him. They want him for more offences than you can name. They think somehow he's situated himself here in Mistletoe or in the area around here."

"And Eavan moved here. Is that a coincidence? I don't think so. Gran said it was suggested to her that Eavan move here but she can't remember who suggested it. I'll ask her again." He looked down at the paperwork he had been perusing when Samuel interrupted him. "I've been working on Eavan's past. I don't like what I'm finding. Her father somehow was connected to that name."

"I was afraid of that. How deep was he?"

"Not deep. I'm sure he didn't know who he was working for. It was a shell company, so he likely never knew the names. It would seem he was on the legitimate side of the company, which is good news for Eavan."

"That's a blessing then, Simon. Now, how do we keep your lady and her Gran safe?"

Simon shot Samuel a quick look at that, but saw only concern on his face. "I have no idea, Samuel. It's going to be difficult as Eavan will just take off looking for photos. And she refuses to carry a phone. She says she can't when she's out looking for nature photos. Even the vibration may be enough to chase away the perfect shot."

"That's not good. Stay with her as much as you can. You need to get through to her somehow."

"I know I do, but we're nowhere near that, Samuel. I can't claim all her time."

"I think you can. I was watching her without either of you knowing it. I've seen her around you. I've seen the way she looks at you, watches you when she thinks you're not looking, that no one can see her. She looks at you with her heart in her eyes and on her face." Samuel paused, letting Simon absorb what he had said. "What I'm saying, Simon, is this. She looks at you as if you're the treasure she's been seeking all her life, after God that is. Don't play with her. Take her trust and build from there." He stood, gathering his thoughts.

Simon waited, knowing his friend had something to add. He took what Samuel said to him gracefully, knowing that was how he felt about Eavan and not quite sure how to continue.

"I see how you watch her, Simon. You haven't seen me behind you when you're looking for her, even though she's not in the crowd. The boys have mentioned that something is different about you right now. This is what it is."

Simon nodded. "I know, Samuel. I hear what you're saying. She is my treasure, my heart. I just don't know how to approach her."

Samuel laughed. "This uncertainty, coming from you, Simon?" He took pity on his friend. "You have seen how Levi is with his Julia, Jacob with Finn, Josh with Leah, Jeremiah with Joy. They all want you to find someone to complete your life. Eavan may be that. She may not be. Be prepared in the event that she does walk away. I sense she has issues that she needs to work through. Not the least is that of her heritage."

Samuel stood for a moment, his eyes on his young friend, his heart lifting in prayer, before he walked away, leaving Simon staring after him.

Simon stared at the closed door, then looked back down at his paperwork, immersing himself in it once more. He finally threw down his pen. He needed a break from this, he had found out too much information that he didn't need to know. He sighed, knowing at some point that day he would need to speak with Samuel, and then Chief Ed Waters of town.

He rose, his feet taking him towards Eavan's studio. He entered, not seeing her, and heading for the living quarters, meeting Megan coming towards him.

"Simon. I didn't expect to see you today." She reached to hug him, considering him family all ready.

"I didn't expect to be here. Is Eavan here?"

Megan shook her head. "No, she's not. She took her camera and said she was heading out about town, needing some urban photos. I'm really not sure where you'd find here." She watched as disappointment flickered across Simon's face.

"So I guess there's not much point in waiting, is there?" He started to laugh, sputtering out an apology.

"So I'm not company enough, is that what you're saying?" Megan laughed at the consternation on his face.

"No, that's not what I meant." He reached to hug her once more. "I'm just worried about Eavan."

"I know you are. Go and find her. Come back for dinner when you have."

Simon searched the stores and shops on the main street, then stood, uncertainty in his manner as to where to look next. He headed towards the park where the tree was waiting to be lit on Saturday for the commencement of the Christmas festivities. Somehow he knew he'd find her there.

A sharp cry caught his attention and he spun, then ran towards the gazebo, sliding to a halt just out of sight. Eavan was there, struggling to release her arm from the heavyset man who held her, her foot coming back to kick him in the shin. He gave a sharp yell, his hand releasing her as he reached for the shin. She spun and ran, heading right for Simon, who caught her in his arms and then headed around the gazebo, her hand tight in his as they ran. He heard the yell of outrage behind him.

He pulled Eavan into his arms once more as he stopped behind a large tree, their breaths coming in heavy gasps. He searched her face, seeing the fear on it, and hating that for her.

He listened as he heard the man running by him, his voice calling for Eavan, saying he would find her and she would regret what she had just done.

Simon waited, finally peeking around the tree and searching the area. He looked down at the lady in his arms and hurt for her. She had finally buried her face against him, fear still shaking her.

"Eavan? Come on, love. Let's get you out of here."

She nodded, finally looking up at him. "I can't go back to the studio but I need to." Somehow, in all that she still had her camera. "I need to process these today." She was hesitant as to what she should do, not at all like her usual decisive self.

Simon watched her face, seeing that for once she needed someone else make a decision for her. He reached to kiss her cheek, her hand coming to the spot, her eyes open in wonder as she stared at him.

"Come on, then, love. Let's get you home and to your studio. I need to talk to you at some point anyway."

"But what about your work? Won't Samuel tell you to go back to the office?"

Simon grinned as he led her away from the trees and back to the centre of town. "Nope. He told me to go find you."

Simon watched as Eavan sorted through the photos, selecting the ones she wanted to work on, and then lost her as she became absorbed in her work. He looked around as Megan tapped at the door and then entered, rising to take the tray from her.

"Eavan. You need to eat something. Come on, love. Set your work aside for a few moments."

Eavan finally heard Simon's voice and looked up, surprised that he was still there. "You stayed?"

"I did. Where else would I be?" He watched as her face softened and then she reached to hug him.

"Thank you. Anyone else would have left by now."

"I find it fascinating what you do. Talk to me about it."

She shrugged. "There's not really much I can say. The programs I use are great. Someone has done a lot of work there that makes my work easier." She paused to bite into her sandwich, chewing and then swallowing. "But you wanted to talk to me. What about?"

Simon wiped his mouth with the cloth napkin Megan had provided, his eyes on it as he fingered the softness of it, trying to gather his thoughts. They always seemed to disappear or disintegrate when he was near Eavan.

"Samuel has come up with a name. Someone your father worked for." He held up his hand as she went to speak. "Just let me say my piece. I only want to say it once and then we'll talk. Samuel's willing to meet with us."

Eavan sat back when Simon finished speaking, shock on her face. "He found out all that. He's good. But how much had you found out?"

"I wasn't looking into that. I was looking at your high school classmates, your college classmates, that kind of things. The teachers, professors."

She shivered. "I don't like that there is so much out there about me. I want to stay private and I can't, now can I?" She sighed. "Now what, Simon? How do I stay safe? I know that's what you're planning."

He nodded. "I am. Listen, come with me tonight. My friends and I meet for a Bible study tonight and I would love to have you join us."

She stared at him for a moment, before she nodded. "I guess. I've already been thrown into the deep end without warning. May as well go out further into the lake."

Simon laughed hard at her phrasing. "Out deeper, you say? Then you'll need someone close to rescue you. Let it be me, please?" His laughter had turned to a gentle smile as he traced a finger down her cheek.

She nodded, not looking at him. "How dressed up is this meeting anyway?"

"Not dressy. We'll be meeting at Jeremiah and Joy's tonight. He's our pastor but Joy is twin to Josh. Joy's parents are away so they can't watch the little girls."

"Gran told me about them, how they were adamant they were sitting with you on Sunday. Be careful there, Simon."

"I always am, love. Those two little girls are so precious."

She clasped his hand tight later as they walked up to the front door of a house. She was really apprehensive, not sure what her reception would be. She still saw Julia's face from the other day, the shock on it.

Simon stopped her, drawing her into a hug before he spoke.

"They will not bite you. I will leave with you if there is anything negative or you feel uncomfortable at any time."

"You can't do that. They're your friends." Eavan was shocked at his words.

"I can and I will. Tonight, you are the most important thing to me, right after God. Do you understand, Eavan?" He waited for her nod, feeling her hair brush against his chin. "I mean exactly what I said. I will leave and they will understand completely if I do. That's the kind of friends they are."

He turned as he heard the door open and Jeremiah stood there, waiting to welcome them.

"Are we going in or are we leaving? The choice is yours and yours alone. I will not force you to do something you're not ready to do yet."

She finally stepped back, her eyes searching his, seeing the sincerity and determination to please her in them. She turned to the door, seeing Jeremiah standing there, waiting for them.

“I’m sorry. I’ve kept you waiting.”

Jeremiah grinned as he reached to shake her hand, then take her jacket as Simon helped her slip it off. “Not at all. We haven’t got started yet.   Joy is having trouble getting the girls to bed. They know Simon’s coming tonight and for some reason they won’t settle until he says good night to them.”

Simon started to laugh. “Sure, make me the scapegoat for disobedience, Jeremiah. Is everyone else here?”

Jeremiah shook his head. “Julia and Blackie are running late. She called with some excuse that I can’t remember off hand.”

Simon laughed again.   “That’s not you.   You know exactly why they’re late. Now, where are your girls?” He turned as he heard the patter of bare feet running towards him, and he bent to pick up the two girls.

“Simon, you came.   Read story.” Holly was adamant that Simon would read the bedtime story that night.

"Not tonight, sweetness.   I have a friend I can't leave on her own."

Heidi peeked over her shoulder at Eavan and waved. "She can come listen to it. We'll let her."

Joy choked on the laughter she was trying to keep from bursting forth. "Say good night, girls. Then, it is off to bed with you. Now, please."

Simon watched as the girls clung to their mother's hands, skipping along happily beside her. He shook his head as he turned to find Eavan's eyes on him, laughter brimming in them.

"I think you have a new name."

"And that would be?"

"The Pied Piper, Simon."

Jeremiah howled with laughter at that as they walked into the sunroom where the other two couples were waiting, Josh and Jacob standing as they saw Eavan.

"Up to no good again, are you, Simon?" Josh laughed at the look Simon shot him.

"Me? Never. Now you, that's another story." Simon laughed at the choruses of agreement from the two women, turning as he felt someone behind him, to find Blackie and Julia standing there.

Eavan stood quietly, feeling very much alone and out of place, knowing the people here had been friends for years and she was the outsider.

Julia stopped, her eyes on Eavan's face as she seemed about ready to run from the room, and then approached her, her hands reaching for Eavan's.

"I owe you a huge apology. I was just so taken aback the other night, I didn't act like I normally would. Welcome to Mistletoe. Welcome to the family."

Eavan stared at Julia, seeing how glad Julia seemed to be to have her there. "Thank you, I think." She shot Simon a glare as he laughed quietly before he came to stand beside her, his arm going around her, bringing comfort and peace to her.

"No. I really mean it. I always wanted a sister, always felt there was someone else belonging to Jonathan and I out there.   Uncle Ben we discovered just about two years ago now. I had known him for years, never knowing he was my uncle. That's how much he had to keep it quiet." She leaned back against Blackie, emotions getting the better of her for a moment.

"Then, thank you, Julia. I appreciate your words." She looked back at Simon, seeing his nod of approval before looking back at Julia. "Gran said she met you on Sunday. That she heard your voice and thought I was there."

"You two do sound somewhat alike, but you have a different lilt to your voice." Leah walked over and hugged Eavan, taking her by surprise. "Welcome to our family, Eavan. Did I say it right? I've been practicing but wasn't sure. I'm a cousin of sorts, related to both Finn and Julia, and now you. This is great. Another female cousin I can do things with."

Josh had approached as well, reaching out to shake Eavan's hand, seeing how overwhelmed she was. "I'm Josh, Leah's husband. Some day, we'll tell you all about how Leah discovered her roots here in town."

"You mean you're not from here?"

Leah shook her head. "Nope. I'm from the other coast or rather was." She turned to Jacob and Finn. "This is Finn and Jacob. Finn has the antiquities' store in town. I hear you're a photographer. She has a really neat display of old cameras and whatnot. You might be interested in that. And this is her husband, Jacob."

They finally sat, Eavan tight to Simon, his arm around her for reassurance, as they started their Bible study. Eavan was surprised that Jeremiah, as the pastor, didn't lead it, but rather Josh did.

Walking out with the group, Eavan suddenly shivered and looked around. Someone was watching her, she could tell,. Just who, she didn't know, but she felt the oncoming danger and knew she had no way to avoid it, not now. She just prayed that Simon would not be around when it hit, knowing he would take the brunt of whatever happened for her.

Josh was watching her, seeing her glancing around, and then looked around himself, knowing what she was feeling. He would need to talk to Simon, he decided, at some point in the next few days. Little did he know he would not have an opportunity before danger struck, involving not just Eavan.

Chapter 9

ɀavan looked up from the studio counter, surprised to see the three woman who walked through her door. She watched as they circled the room, studying her photos before Julia approached her.

"Eavan, forgive us for just dropping in. We've been passing this studio for days now, saying we needed to pop in, not realizing it was yours."

Eavan smiled. "No one does, not unless they're told. I've done that on purpose, to keep my personal and professional lives separate."

"Simon told us about the mouse photo. I would love to see it sometime." Leah had approached. "I didn't know it was you Mom had hired to take Rebecca's pictures. We are always asked who the photographer is, they are just exquisite. You captured her so perfectly."

Eavan blushed. "Thank you. She was so precious to photograph. Now, what can I get you ladies? Gran's out, Maggie's not due in today, so it's just me. I have tea, I think coffee, juice, water."

"We're fine, Eavan. It's you we came to see." Finn had walked up to the counter as well. "Any chance you could get away for lunch?"

Eavan shook her head. "Unfortunately, not today. I have to stay here, I think."

"Well, in that case, I'll be right back." Leah headed for the door.

Finn and Julia started to laugh at the look on Eavan's face.

"Don't worry. She's just heading to Josh's restaurant and will be back with lunch for us." Finn took pity on Eavan. "Josh owns The House."

"Oh, he does? We love his food, Gran and I, when we do dine out and that's not often."

Eavan looked up later, her attention briefly distracted from the conversation going on around her. She frowned as she heard the door click in the back of building, then shrugged, thinking it was Gran that had come back earlier than she had planned. Her attention was caught again by Finn's words.

Julia looked up at a sound, fear suddenly showing on her face, as she shoved back her chair and rose. The other three women were startled and then spun as a male voice could be heard.

"So, I finally catch you, Eavan Walker. It's taken years." The man standing near her was younger, but heavy, a weapon held in his right hand trained on her.

Eavan's heart quaked within her, recognizing one of the voices that had tormented her for so many years. Lord, protect these ladies with me. I don't care about me, but don't let any harm come to them.

"Jeff Young. So it's been you all along. Where's your boss? Or are you acting on your own?"

A cruel laugh exploded from him as another man entered the studio and stood just inside the door, his own weapon trained on the women.

Lord, we could use some help right about now, Eavan prayed, but it looks as if it's just us and them. Guide me, Lord, in what I need to do. Grant me the courage and strength to win over this monster. Keep the ladies safe and unharmed.

She listened to the man rant and rave, knowing he was speaking for his employer, a man she had never met but who had made her life miserable for years. At least, that's who she thought it had been.

She finally saw an opportunity, a crack in his demeanour, a chance she just had to take. She shared a look with Leah, who nodded. Of all the women, Leah seemed to understand her the best. Perhaps it was because of what she had been through, but she knew what it was like to be uncertain, to not know who her own family was.

She rose and began to pace her studio, seeming not to watch the man, but keeping her eye on him. He turned to follow her, his weapon now down at his side, his finger off the trigger. She shot a glance at the man near the door and saw his weapon had been holstered, which didn't make a lot of sense. Not unless they were waiting for someone to come, and just who that was, she had no idea and had no intention of letting in the studio.

She turned once more, finding him close to her. His hand came out and struck her across the face, drawing blood from her lip and leaving a red mark on her cheek. She blinked back tears before her eyes shot to the women, watching them closely, seeing Leah's nod. She spun, her booted foot shooting out to connect with the side of his knee, bringing a loud cry from him as they heard cracking of bones and saw him fall, his weapon dropping from his head and sliding a few feet away. Eavan dove for the weapon, grasping it before she rose, training it on the man near the door, who had pulled his own weapon, directing it at her. She waited, not sure for what, seeing Leah standing with her foot ground onto the man's hand, her full weight on his fingers, as he shouted and screamed for her to move. Julia had her phone out, calling for help, even as Finn stood, watching, ready to step in where she needed to.

Finn watched in fascination as a heavy oak walking stick cracked down on the man's wrist, sending his weapon flying, and heard his screams of pain. Megan appeared behind him, brandishing the walking stick.

"That will teach you, you ruffian. Don't ever think you'll get away with threatening my granddaughter or her friends." She peered around him at Eavan. "You're okay, love?"

"I am, Gran, thanks to you. Ladies, meet my Gran. Gran, Leah, Julia and Finn there by the door. Where did you come from anyway?"

"God told me I needed to come home, so I did. I cut my shopping short, and now thanks to these two ruffians, I'll be needing to go out again to finish."

"Not today, Gran. Not today. You'll not be allowed to."

Finn spun as the door was flung open and heavily armed police officers swarmed in. Once they had been assured the women were safe, the men were handcuffed, before the paramedics were allowed in. Ed Waters directed them to the women first, despite the complaints of the two men.

"You'll be looked at. The women come first." Ed studied the five women, his eyes lingering on Eavan, before he nodded. He knew her, he thought, but how he couldn't quite remember. He would, likely the memory waking him up in the middle of the night.

One by one, the woman gave their statements and were then escorted from the building, their eyes searching for their husbands standing behind the police lines, their steps breaking into a run before they were caught in their men's arms and then hurried away by the police.

Simon stood, waiting, fear running through him as the paramedics were in no hurry to come out. He watched as men in handcuffs were led from the building, his attention going back to the door. Finally Tom, an officer he knew well, approached him.

"Simon? The chief asked if you would come with me." He smiled at the apprehension on Simon's face. "It's okay. Your lady's fine. She's just finishing up her statement as is her grandmother." He pointed. "There. Her grandmother is done. The chief said Jeremiah or Samuel would take care of her."

Simon stopped by Megan, before hugging her, smiling briefly at her complaints.

"I have groceries I need to put away, Simon. Will you look after that for me? And they tell me we can't come back tonight. That's not suitable."

"Don't worry, Megan. Samuel here will look after you. His wife will make sure you have what you need."

She grumbled as Samuel tucked her arm into his elbow and led her away, the police tape lifting briefly to let them through.

Simon stood in the door of the studio, seeking the disarray from the afternoon, the photos that had been torn from the wall, the glass and frames smashed. He saw the remnants of the women's lunches dropped on the hardwood floor. He saw the debris from the paramedics as they had treated the wounded men. Who he did not see was Eavan, but he could hear her, her voice calm but taut.

Tom nodded to him as he moved. "Go on back, Simon. She's just finishing up.

She needs you, the chief says, and the chief is never wrong."

Simon gave a small tight smile even as he headed for the living quarters, sidestepping the techs at work. He would need to find cleaners, he decided, not wanting either Megan or Eavan to clean up the mess.

He stood, his eyes on his lady, seeing the stress and strain she had been under. He couldn't see her face, but her stance as she stood talking with the chief said more than she could.

She finally turned, and he drew in his breath sharply, seeing the bruising on her face, the blood from the cut on her swollen lip.

Eavan stood, shocked to see Simon standing there, but glad, knowing he was just who she needed. She ignored the chief as she swiftly crossed to Simon, to be enveloped in a hard tight hug, one that said he would never let her go and that he was sorry he had not been there.

She didn't hear his quiet words to the chief or the chief's response, just felt him as he shifted to draw off his coat and wrap it around her, his arm around her as well as he led her through the back door and down the streets at the back, her steps stumbling at times. He finally sighed, swept her into his arms and headed for Samuel's place, just a few blocks away.

Blackie's mother, Mirian, waited at the door, her arms going out to hug Eavan. She turned, her arm still around the younger woman.

"Come, love. Let's get you cleaned up. Rachel or Rebecca will have some clothes that will fit you. They're tall like you are. Simon, Samuel's in the kitchen with Megan."

Simon watched as Eavan looked back at him, fear on her face. He nodded towards Miriam.

"She'll take care of you. Trust her. She's been through this with Blackie and Julia."

"You have?" Eavan's attention went to Miriam.

"I have, and I pray that I don't have to with my two girls. My heart just can't take that."

Simon stood for a moment, gathering his thoughts. He grew determined in what he needed to do. Now he just had to convince Eavan of what he wanted. Lord, don't let me rush ahead of You. That I do not want to do. Guide my steps and my words.

Simon was on a hunt a few hours later. Even though it was early, Megan had declared she had had enough excitement for the day and retired. Rachel and Rebecca had moved in together for the next few days, something they were willing and glad to do for their Simon, as they called him, thinking of him as a beloved big brother. Eavan had been avoiding him since they had eaten and he wanted to know why.

"Eavan? What's wrong, love?" Simon stood in front of her where she stood near the French doors of the sun room. "Talk to me."

"I have to leave, Simon. I brought this trouble to your friends. They could have been killed because of me."

"No one blames you, love. No one at all. They know where the blame lies and it isn't with you." He moved closer, his hands on her upper arms. "Please, don't leave. My heart couldn't take it if you did."

She shook her head, sorrow on her face. "I have to, Simon. I can't have someone hurt because of me."

"I can tell you right now someone would be hurt if you do leave. I would be. My heart would never recover." He reached to draw her close, finding her resisting him, and sighed. His hand came up to cup her cheek, his thumb lightly touching the cut on her lip. "I hate that he did this to you. And it wasn't even the one after you. Just one of his henchman."

"His top one, I would imagine. He would send no one else, you know. That's the character of the man who has been chasing me now for years."

Simon nodded, his eyes on her face. "I know, love. I know that. We're gathering information on him. Samuel has pulled men and women off other investigations just for this."

“He shouldn’t.”

“Well, he has.   It was his decision. I’ve been working on your side of it. He’s working on who is behind it.”   Simon hugged her tighter, his chin on the top of her head. “My heart couldn’t take it if you left.”

She shoved against him.   “And just what do you mean by that?” She stood back from him, her eyes unbelieving as she stared at him.   “Tell me.   Exactly what do you mean.”

Simon sighed to himself once again. This was not how he wanted to tell her she had his heart, that she was the one he had been waiting for all his life. “It’s like this, love.   You have my heart, have had since you called me an oaf out there in the forest.” He watched as her eyes widened in disbelief before they narrowed once again. “I’m in love with you, Eavan. I have been since the first time I saw you.   Don’t leave me, please.”

She shook her head. “You can’t. Not so soon.   It just doesn’t happen that way. Not in real life. Only in books and movies.”

Simon smiled at her even as he drew her back to him. "It does, love. It did with me. Just let me know if you'll accept my suit, as my grandmother would say."

He finally felt her nod. Thank You, Lord. Now, don't let me screw this up, please. They stood for a while longer before he bent and kissed the bruise on her cheek, turning her towards the main part of the house.

"You need your rest, love. Sleep well. I'll be bunked down here in Samuel's office. I'm not leaving you alone, not any more."

She stood for a moment, her eyes on his face before she reached and pulled his head down, placing a kiss on his cheek.

"Good night, you big oaf." She had turned her words into an endearment and he loved her for that.

Chapter 10

$\mathcal{T}$wo days later, Eavan looked up from her monitor, her eyes needing the break. She had been hard at work, trying to meet her deadlines that were closing in on her, having missed a day's work when she was assaulted and the ladies she was coming to know had been put at risk. Her sight landed on Simon, sitting at a desk near her, his attention on his laptop as he researched. What he was working on, he wouldn't or couldn't tell her. He would just laugh at her when she told him he needed to, he was working in her office.

Simon glanced up, catching her watching him, and then sat back from his work. "Almost done, love?"

She nodded, happiness flowing through her. "This is the last one I have pending and I just sent the proofs off. I just need to wait for their decisions and then send the copies they requested." She glanced at his laptop. "How about you?"

"I'm done for the day, too. I have to wait for responses to emails and queries I sent off. That will take a few days." He rose, walking over to perch on the corner of her desk, his eyes assessing her. "Now what?"

"Now what?" She shrugged. "I have no idea. Gran is deep in baking, I think she said, for the afternoon. She is insisting that she has to provide Irish goodies to all your friends. Trust me. They'll love them and want the recipes. That they will never get. I can't even get some of them."

He laughed at the aggrieved tone in her voice. "I'm sure she'll give them to you some day."

A voice spoke from the doorway. "I'll give them to you, Simon, and teach you how to bake them, as long as you promise not to share the recipes." Megan and Simon both began to laugh at the squeal of fake rage that came from Eavan. "What I wanted to ask you, Simon, was if you would let me take you out for a meal, to that restaurant of your friend's? I feel like I need to do something for you, you've done so much for me."

Simon stood, reaching to drop a kiss on Megan's cheek. "I don't need payment for what I've done, you know that.   I consider you family and family doesn't need to be paid back."

"I know that, Simon. Just humour me, okay."   She patted his cheek before she hurried away, her voice carrying back to them. "Now, hurry up and shut down what you need to.   I've made reservations for thirty minutes from now.   I spoke to someone named Amy, I think it was."

Simon stared after her before he felt Eavan's finger under his chin, shutting his mouth.

"What's the surprise there, Simon?"

"Josh doesn't do reservations. At least he never has in the past." Simon shook his head, not sure what he was walking into but willing to do anything for his Eavan and her beloved Gran.

Josh watched from the kitchen as Simon escorted Megan and Eavan to a table that Amy had set specifically for them. She had approached him after Megan had called, asking for a reservation for that night. He had stared at her, stating they didn't do reservations.

"I know that, Josh." Amy had begun to laugh, but tears sparkled in her eyes, giving away her tender heart directed towards her employer and his friends. "I just couldn't say no to her. She's so sweet."

Amy stopped beside Josh as he stood. "Well, what did you come up with for dinner for them? And don't say you didn't plan something special. I know you."

He laughed. "I did. It's a good thing there aren't many people in the restaurant. We'd have a revolt on our hands. Here, take out their salads. Their main course will be a few minutes."

Simon watched the two women who had become special in his life enjoy their meal, knowing he didn't want the evening to end but it would at some point. He caught sight of Josh moving around the kitchen and nodded at his wave. Josh and Amy were up to something, he thought, but what he had no idea.

Megan stood and went to find Amy, saying she had to talk to Josh, she wanted to thank him for their meal. Eavan looked after her, then back at Simon.

"That's not Gran. She doesn't do that."

Simon laughed. "Well, tonight she did." He reached for Eavan's hand. "I'm glad she left us on our own for a moment." He hesitated, uncertainty seen his face.

"Simon?" Eavan's quiet voice drew his eyes to her face.

"Eavan, I know we're relative strangers, but you know my heart. You know I love you. Will you trust me and take it one step farther? Will you be mine for life, for however long God gives us? If you don't want to answer now, if you need time, it's fine."

Eavan sat there, tears welling in her eyes. Only Simon, Lord, she thought, would ask me to marry him in the middle of such uncertainty and danger, and in the middle of a restaurant. She was unable to speak, nodding instead, her love for him in her eyes and on her face.

Simon drew a breath of relief, raising her hand to kiss it. "When we're alone, I'll do better than kiss your hand. Thank you, love. God knows our hearts. He knows how long we have with each other. All we can do is trust Him and each other."

He stood as Megan came back, followed by Josh, who eyed the couple, then shook his head. Something had changed but he wasn't sure what. Lord, You alone know.

Simon drew Eavan into her studio, the lights on low as she usually left them. He could hear Megan singing softly to herself. He traced Eavan's face with his hand before he cupped her chin and bent and kissed her. Her hands came up to grasp his, not willing to let him go. He then stood, his forehead on hers, his eyes closed before he spoke.

"Tomorrow, we find your ring and then talk to Jeremiah. I hope you don't want a long engagement."

"Oh, I think a year or two might be best." She giggled as he stared in disbelief at her before he began to laugh and swept her into his arms.

"You had me going there, love. We'll need to tell Gran."

"Tell Gran what?" They jumped as they heard her voice behind them. "That you two are in love? That's been obvious for days. When is the wedding? Soon, I hope."

Megan reached to hug the two of them, her head bowed in prayer as she spoke a blessing on them, asking God's protection and provisions for them.

Simon stood, his arms around both women. "We need to speak with Jeremiah. I have no idea how soon for the wedding. I know Josh and Leah married in less than a week. Julia and Blackie and Finn and Jacob took longer."

"Not a long time, I think, Simon." Eavan looked up at him. "Somehow, I think we're not done with what's his name and that our time is precious."

"That is it. What about a dress and all those doodads?" Simon looked down at Megan as she slapped his arm, laughing as she moved away.

"I have her mother's dress packed away. It will fit her well, I'm thinking. As for the doodads, the baking is done. She'll need flowers, and that's your task, my boy."

Eavan shook her head as she watched her Gran move away. "We've been told, Simon. Now that's settled, where do we live? Here or at your place?"

"My place, I think. There is an in-law suite with its own private entrance that would be perfect for Gran. She'd be close but we'd all have our privacy. Would that work?"

"It will work just fine, my boy." Gran's voice behind him made him jump. She laughed in glee at having surprised him for a second time in just minutes. "Get used to me, boy. You'll have me around for years."

Simon reached to hug her, not having had a grandparent in his life for many years, and loving the idea of Gran being part of their lives.

He paused later as he opened his front door, his hand reaching into the mail box, and pulling out the mail. He dropped it on his office desk before he headed for his bedroom and the jewelry box his mother had left him. He searched through it, finding the rings he knew where there. Would Eavan accept either one, or would she want new?

Simon fingered his mail late that night, then walked away from it. It could wait. He headed for the door to the in-law suite, unlocking it and then flipping on lights as he moved through it. It was furnished, had been for months, he thought. He would bring Eavan and Gran over the next night and let them decide on any changes they wanted to make. And make changes he was determined they would make. He wanted a home for both of them, not just a place to live.

Eavan looked with interest around his home the next night, Gran having headed for the suite that would be hers. She could Gran and Simon talking, Gran determined to leave everything like it was, Simon just as determined she would make the place a home for herself.

She turned from the back door and glanced around the kitchen, liking the light wood on the cupboards and yellow, oranges, rusts and brown Simon had incorporated into the backsplash and countertop. She was glad he had not gone for stainless appliances. She disliked them immensely but had no idea why.

Simon stood watching her, his heart in his eyes, before he moved towards her.

"Eavan?" When she turned, he kissed her, then stood where he was, with Eavan captured in his arms.

"I like your house, Simon. It's comfortable. I don't see what you want me to change."

He sighed, knowing he hadn't worded it right. "I want you to make it into a real home, your home. Just like I want Gran to make the suite her home."

"And we'll do that, Simon." Gran stood watching them. "It just won't be overnight. You have to live in a house to feel its bones, to feel what it wants to tell you, to find out how to decorate." She looked around. "You have done that. Your tastes are so similar to Eavan, it's spooky."

Eavan laughed at her Gran. "They are, aren't they? Now we just have to decide what we want to bring. I think we'll leave the apartment we're in furnished. We'll need supplies there anyway."

Simon hugged her tight to him. "I am so glad." He turned her to the office. "Now, if Gran will excuse us for a moment, I have something I need to ask you, in private, sort of."

"Well, that's definite, isn't it, Simon?" Gran made a shooing motion. "Go on and then come back. I'll find some food for us. I know Simon has tea. I already peeked."

Eavan had drawn her breath at the two rings Simon had presented to her, choosing the emerald in its simple setting, saying it would be an honour to wear his mother's ring. He had kissed her soundly for that before they returned to the kitchen, where Gran waited to see the ring Eavan presented to her.

Gran's eyes gleamed with tears as she hugged her granddaughter. She was happy for her but fearful at the same time, knowing danger still surrounded them.

Chapter 11

*S*imon grabbed up the mail from his home desk the next morning, intent on getting to the office. His lieutenant had called, asking him to call once he was in. He had information for him that he thought Simon could use.

Simon dropped the mail on the desk, intent on making that call, until the mail slid sideways and a plain envelope caught his attention. He scanned it, seeing the name of a lawyer in the corner and then frowned.

Samuel stood for a moment in the hallway, watching Simon. He had been on his way to his own office but stopped as he saw Simon just standing there.

"Simon? Is something wrong?"

Looking up, Simon shrugged. "I'm not sure, Samuel. I found this letter in the mail from home. It's from a lawyer I don't know."

"Then, boot up your computer and see what you can find out. Let me know. I would be interested in what that letter contains. If you don't mind sharing, that is."

Simon nodded, his eyes on his computer monitor as he typed in the name of the lawyer, growing as he saw who it was.

"Now, why would they be contacting me?"

He slit the envelope open, not seeing the small envelope containing a minute amount of power. Before he could even draw the letter from the envelope, he began to have difficulty breathing. The sound of his body hitting the floor had his work mates running for his office, Samuel shoving by them to drop on his knees beside the young man, calling for paramedics and the police.

Samuel felt for a pulse, all the while looking around, seeing the open envelope and the spying the small envelope inside it, both slit open with the letter opener.

"Here, give me a hand. Out to the reception area. And close that door. No one comes in here." Samuel gently laid Simon's head down, afraid for him as he saw the struggle to breathe. He prayed for his young friend as he moved back, letting the paramedics in to work on Simon.

The paramedics struggled to work on Simon, desperate to keep him breathing.

"What happened?" One of them looked up even as he reached for the leads to the heart monitor.

"He opened an envelope. I wasn't there but there was a little envelope in the big one. I think he's been drugged." Samuel ran his hands through his hair, knowing exactly what he was saying.

"Drugged? As in overdose?" The paramedics worked even harder, one reaching for the kit they carried just for overdoses.

Samuel watched as they finally stabilized Simon enough to move him to a stretcher, preparatory to moving him to the hospital. He watched as they slid the breathing tube in, and started the IV. He turned.

"I'm going to find Eavan. Call me when the police are done." He was out the door, running for his car, his phone in his hand. "Blackie, I need you and Julia at the hospital. Simon's down and I'm heading for Eavan. No. I'm not sure what happened." He listened to Blackie's question even as he heard Blackie calling for Julia. "An overdose somehow. The police will sort out that. Eavan will need someone with her."

Eavan had looked up as Samuel stood in her office doorway, his breath in gasps as he asked her to come with him. She had thrown down her pen, grabbed her jacket, calling to Gran that Simon was hurt and that she'd call. Megan and Maggie had stood, arms around one another, as they watched Samuel drive away.

Eavan paced the waiting room and had been since Samuel ushered her in. It had been three hours since Simon collapsed and they were still working on him. Eavan didn't know that he had been close to death more than once. They had finally found the drug that he had inhaled without knowing and found the antidote that was needed. The paramedics' quick work on the scene had kept him alive long enough for that to happen.

She turned as she felt an arm come around her. Julia stood there, compassion on her face before she hugged her sister, Blackie's arms coming around the two ladies, his face raised in prayer for his friend. Those two and Josh and Jacob had served in the service together, becoming fast friends, going their own way on discharge, but reuniting again in Mistletoe. Each man had been sent there, why and who was still in a cloud, even though Jacob's lawyer had been behind part of it, before he ended up in prison himself.

Doc stood for a moment, his eyes on the three in the middle of the waiting room, before roaming the room and seeing Simon's friends gathered, Jeremiah standing near the door where he could watch all them. Doc knew he would be in prayer, having gotten to know him well at church.

Doc's eyes came back to the two ladies as they separated, hands wiping at their faces. He paused as he saw the ring on Eavan's finger, knowing that Samuel was right, Simon had made his choice and put his ring on his lady's finger. He thanked God that Simon was still alive, but not conscious. That worried Doc.

Blackie turned at that moment, seeing Doc standing there. Julia saw his movement and turned Eavan towards the physician, introducing her to him.

"Doc? How is he?"

"Very fortunate, Eavan. May I call you that? Simon is a good friend." She nodded and then he continued. "We have him stabilized for now and are moving him up to an ICU bed. He is on a heart monitor, kidney dialysis, and on a ventilator. We need to keep him quiet for now and let the medications we are treating him with do their work. Come. Let me take you back to him. You do want to go, don't you?" He asked the question as she hesitated.

Samuel moved forward, his arm coming around Eavan. "Let me go with you, Eavan. That is, if it's okay with Doc." Doc nodded, grateful that Samuel had stepped in just as he would have with Julia or with one of his own two girls. He knew Samuel thought of Simon as another son and would do just about anything for him.

Eavan stood for a moment, overwhelmed by the sounds of the monitors and the ventilator, her eyes not able to take in all that was in the room before they fell to Simon. With a subdued cry, she was across the room, bending over the stretcher to touch his face, careful of the equipment attached to him. She reached to kiss his forehead, then found his hand, not liking the coldness of it, nor its laxity.

She stood for how long she didn't know before the nurses walked towards her, gently moving her to one side as they moved the stretcher and equipment that was needed. Simon was heading for an ICU unit, still alive but not aware that his love stood near, frozen in her despair. Samuel caught her hand and led her after the stretcher, Miriam appearing beside her, her arm wrapped around the younger woman. Megan, Samuel knew, had arrived and been taken to the waiting room upstairs.

Eavan stood once more at Simon's bedside, not knowing when he would arouse. Doc had been confident that he would, but just when was uncertain. She turned as she felt Gran's hand on her back and then clung to her grandmother, tears falling silently down her cheeks.

Gran let her cry, in her wisdom knowing it was needed before she spoke.

"The police chief is here, child. He wants to talk to you."

"I can't leave him, Gran."

"You can and you will. The nurses have said you need to. They'll come get you when you can come back in."

Ed looked up as Gran came back with Eavan. He was shocked at the devastation he saw on Eavan's face, even though Samuel had warned him the younger couple had become engaged.

"Eavan? Come, sit with me please. I do need to talk with you." Ed waited until she had found a seat, her hand in her grandmother's. "I'm not sure what you have been told, but Simon opened an envelope he had received at home at the office. Thank God he didn't open it at home. We wouldn't be sitting here having this conversation if we had."

Eavan winced and then nodded. "What was in that envelope?"

"We've sent it to the lab. We know it was a drug of some kind and the hospital was able to determine what it was and find the antidote. There was a letter inside as well. I don't have a copy, but it threatened Simon. Just why, that's what we're working on. It doesn't seem to have anything to do with you, before you ask."

She sat back, relief in her motions. "I was afraid it did. But who?"

"That's what we are working on. Samuel has pulled some of his people to do that. Simon's fellow detectives are working on that as well. So are mine. We'll find out who it was." He paused, swallowing hard. "I understand you two are engaged. Is that correct?" At her nod, he continued. "We will need to take precautions with you as well. Given the attempts on your life already and now this, I don't think it's safe for you to go back to your studio. Maggie has agreed to work it and I am putting an officer into the living quarters at the back, rotating every twelve hours. As for you two, we'll put you somewhere safe."

Eavan was shaking her head. "Put Gran somewhere safe. I'm not leaving Simon. Not for one moment." She was on her feet and away from Ed before he could stop her.

Megan gave a short laugh. "That's what you will face, Ed, if you even try to remove her. She'll run and hide somewhere here in the hospital, staying close to her love. That's a given. It's who she is."

Ed grinned at Megan, shaking his head. "That's about what I figured. I have officers here that will be on duty at all times. The county force is sending in some as well. We'll do our best to keep them safe. Now, what about you?"

"I won't go anywhere, Ed. I'll stay right here. She needs me, now more than at any time in her life. She's just found a sister and a brother, found out she's related to the town founding families, and that has thrown her world upside down. Throw into the mix someone wanting her hurt or dead, or whatever it is he wants. Then add a brand new love. Like I said, her world is upside down."

"It is at that. Now about that person who is after her. What do you know about that?"

"Not much. I gave Simon the copies of what I had been sent. The same as was sent to her. He said he had taken it to Samuel, so Samuel may be able to help you out there."

"I'll talk to him. We need to pool our resources. I'm sure he's found out more than I have." Ed sat for a moment, fatigue weighing him down, before he rose and walked away.

Megan sat watching him, before she looked up. Samuel and Miriam stood there, their eyes down the hall, a frown on Samuel's face. Megan rose and walked to the hallway, seeing Eavan slumped to the floor, her head on her knees, arms wrapped around her legs, and rushed to her, dropping to her knees.

"Eavan? What's wrong, child?"

Eavan looked up, a stark look on her face, fear in her eyes. "He took a turn for the worse, Gran. They don't know if he'll survive. What will I do if he doesn't?"

Gran sat, wrapping her arms around her beloved granddaughter. "Pray like you never have before, child. That's what will bring him through. God knows what you're going through. He is there."

"It sure doesn't feel like it." Eavan's face went down on her knees again. "I don't know what I'll do if he doesn't make it."

Samuel finally reached and drew Eavan to her feet, then arm around her, led her back to the waiting room and to a chair. Gran sat on one side of her, Miriam on the other, their arms around the younger woman. Samuel crouched in front of her, reaching for her hands even as he prayed. He finally looked at Eavan.

"Jeremiah's called in the church to pray. Someone will be in the prayer room there, twenty hour hours a day until he's out of danger. Trust me on that, Eavan. It's what we do."

She nodded, her eyes finally going past him to look down the hall. "What if he doesn't make it? What do I do?"

"That's not a question we can answer for you. Only God can. But I have every confidence that God will hear your prayers and answer them. Simon has too much to give to the world yet to be taken home."

She finally nodded, then worked herself free from the two older woman, rising to go and stand in the hallway, leaning against the wall, her eyes trained on Simon's cubicle, watching as the nurses moved in and out, gradually making her way down the hall until she stood at the doorway. Looking around, she finally walked towards him, her eyes first on the monitors, then on his face, seeing the dark stubble that was partially covered and reaching her hand out to lay it on his cheek, bending over to kiss his forehead, resting her cheek against his.

The nurse found her that way and paused, knowing she should make her leave, but not having the heart to do that. She turned instead, asking one of the male orderlies to find her a chair for Eavan. She gently shoved Eavan down in the chair, not breaking Eavan's hold on Simon's hand. Finding Eavan's skin chilly, she headed for the supply closet, returning with a warmed sheet that she wrapped around her. She knew Simon from church and from around town, her prayer rising with those of her fellow Christians.

The man who had sent the letter stood near the waiting room, observing and listening to the quiet conversation. He hadn't meant for Simon to die, not just yet. He still had plans he needed to work out before he wreaked his final plot to destroy Simon. That included Eavan now, he decided. Eavan had no idea that there were now two parties after her, both for their own reasons, but she wouldn't have cared if she had known. She had put her trust in God and her hand in Simon's. She was where she needed to be.

Chapter 12

*F*inally opening his eyes, Simon squinted, not quite sure where he was. He stared around, seeing the medical monitors and then reached for the ventilator tube, not liking the feeling of it down his throat. A hand stopped him. He heard voices around him but darkness claimed him again, and this time it was sleep, not unconsciousness that drove him to darkness.

Eavan stood, her hand on Simon's, relieved that he had awakened, but distressed that he had slipped away on her again. She wanted him awake, to look into his eyes, and see that he was healing.

Doc stood watching for a moment before he moved forward, his words quiet to the nurses. Eavan was escorted from the room and told she would be allowed back in later.

The officer assigned to her walked with her to the waiting room, watching as she sat, not alert at all to who was around her. Megan reached out a hand and Eavan took it.

"He was awake, Gran. He opened his eyes. They said he is in a natural sleep now."

"That's good news, then, love. Let the staff do what they need to. You just sit here and put your head back. You need to sleep more than you have in the last few days."

Eavan nodded, even as she yawned, fatigue claiming her. She curled up, her head going down on her Gran's knee and she slept. Doc found them that way later, and stopped, heading back for a blanket that he used to cover Eavan, before he sat beside Megan.

"Doc? How is our boy?" Megan kept her voice low.

"Better. He's been awake again. We've been able to pull the tube, so he's breathing on his own. It's a miracle, Megan. He should not have survived. I thought for a while we'd lose him."

"So did I. God had other plans, Doc, plans that He hasn't shared with us yet."

Doc gave a low laugh. "No, He has not done that. I took the liberty of calling Jeremiah, to pass on the good news. He still has a long road ahead of him, but he is on the mend." Doc shot a look at the officer standing here. "How long do they have guards on them?"

Megan shrugged. "I have no idea. Ed hasn't said, but he did say they haven't caught either party yet, not quite sure who they are." She looked down at Eavan as she stroked her hair. "Eavan knows who's after her. She hasn't said. Who's after Simon, that I have no idea."

Doc sighed, knowing he needed to move on to another patient, but not willing to walk away. He had gotten to know Megan over the past few days and enjoyed his conversations with her, her wit and wisdom adding to his day.

Eavan finally roused, sitting up and pushing her hair back. She rose, heading for Simon, not seeing the man who was following her, behind the officer. She stopped for a moment, to gather her thoughts. It was night, she saw. She had slept most of the day but was still really tired.

She paused, just inside the door, seeing that some of the monitors had been removed. That she was glad to see. Her feet carried her to the bedside, her hand reaching for Simon's, finding him asleep. At least he's not on the ventilator any more, she thought. Her hand traced his cheek, and he turned his head slightly to trap her hand under his face. She smiled.

Lord, I have no idea where the investigation stands, nor do I really want to know. It is enough that Simon is still here, still alive. She stood for the longest time before she finally gave in to her fatigue and curled up beside him, her head on his pillow, his hand clasped tight in hers.

The night nurse found her like that later, reaching to rouse her, then pulling her hand back. What would it hurt, she asked herself, and instead reached for a blanket, covering Eavan before moving to check Simon's vitals. He was almost out of danger she thought, and who would have thought that even that morning. She was not a believer but decided that she needed to look into this faith this family seemed to have.

She turned from the bed, not seeing the man standing in the darkness in the corner, his eyes on the couple, anger and even rage on his face. He needed to reach them, for his boss, but there just didn't seem to be an opportunity.

Simon stirred in the early morning hours, his eyes opening and staying open this time. He searched the room, a frown in place, seeing the monitors by his bed. His hand raised to his face, feeling the nasal prongs bringing oxygen to his lungs, then dropped to his chest, feeling the leads to the heart monitor. He lifted his hand again, staring at the IV line, following it to the to pole and frowning again at the sight of a small bag hanging there as well. He had no memory of the last few days and that scared him. What had happened?

He tried to move and felt a hand tightening on his other hand. He tried to turn his head and realized then that someone's head was beside him. He tilted his head, studying the auburn curls and then following a line of sight to his hand, seeing his hand clasped tightly in her hand, an emerald ring sparkling on her finger.

That's Mom's ring, he thought. Now, how did she get it? Lord, what did I go and do now? He turned as he felt a hand on his shoulders. The night nurse stood there, a smile on her face.

"How are you feeling, Simon?" Her voice was low but comforting.

"Horrible would be how I would describe it. What happened?" He swallowed hard and ran his tongue around his mouth, the dryness preventing him from speaking properly. He drank from the glass the nurse held for him.

"You had a spot of trouble, I would say. Someone tried to kill you. You ended up here." She nodded at Eavan. "She has refused to leave your side. You're a lucky man, Simon, to be loved that much. She was determined you would not die on her, she said, and I would say her prayers worked. Hers and those of your friends."

He nodded, lost for a moment in thought, his face tilting so he could study Eavan, not really recognizing her. His mind was foggy and it hurt to think. He drifted off again.

Eavan finally sat up, her eyes blinking against the early morning light, seeking Simon's face. She slipped from her spot next to him and headed for the door. She knew someone would be waiting for her in the room down the hall and she had to speak with her Gran.

Megan roused as Eavan's hand touched her shoulder.

"Eavan? How is he?"

"Better, I think, Gran. I heard him talking with the nurse earlier but was too tired to rouse properly." Tears sparkled on her lashes. "I don't know that he remembers me though. Doc warned me about that."

"He did at that, love, but he also said it would only be temporary. Simon's system shut down part way to protect him and to let him heal. He'll not have forgotten you." She looked around Eavan as she heard steps coming towards them.

Ed stood for a moment. He had stopped in on his way to the office, having been called in early for another matter. He had news that had come in overnight that he needed to share with Eavan.

"Ed? You're here early." Megan watched Eavan's face pale even more.

"I am, Megan. Eavan, how are you today?" He grinned as she shook her head. "That good, are you? I heard Simon has been awake and talking with the nurse."

Eavan nodded. "He has been, Ed, but he has little memory of what happened."

"We didn't think he would. But that's not why I'm here. I have news." He paused, watching Eavan compose herself. "We identified who sent the envelope to Simon. It has nothing to do with you, and everything to do with his inheritance here in Mistletoe. We're still working on that, to actually determine what all is involved there."

"He is a descendant, isn't he?" Eavan's question caught Ed's attention.

"He is, there is no doubt about that. Just as you are. We're working through what you've told us as well. We want these people responsible for hurting both of you.

You're family, Eavan, you and Simon, and yes, you, Megan."

Ed finally rose and walked away, heading for the office, and a busy day he knew. Eavan watched him go, then rose, not saying a word to her Gran as she paced back to Simon's room.

She stood at his bedside as she had for so many hours, her hand reaching for his hand, finding it warm this time, not cold as it had been for so long. She sank down into her chair as she thought of it, her head bowed in prayer.

Simon had roused as he felt her take his hand and controlled the jump he almost gave at being touched. His head turned slightly, and he watched as she prayed, a small frown on his face. He knew her but could not remember how close they were. It would seem close, given she was wearing that ring, but he needed to talk to her, and he just wasn't sure how to broach the subject.

His hand moved and Eavan looked up, her hand tightening on his, a smile breaking out on her face and lighting up her eyes.

“Simon, you’re awake. Thank God for that.”

Simon frowned. “I’m sorry. I just can’t remember.”

“That’s okay. Doc said that would likely be the case. Whatever drug they hit you with has that side effect. Well, one, anyway.”

He nodded. “I just need to refresh my memory, I think. It’s foggy. How long?”

“Four days since you collapsed in the office. Samuel was there right away, and got you help. If you had opened that letter at home, you wouldn’t be here. You needed help that quickly.”

He nodded, knowing the truth she was speaking. “And I’m sorry, I just can’t remember your name, and I should.” He held up her hand. “It looks as if we’re a couple, and couple should know their partner’s name.”

She smiled even as her free hand came to brush the hair from his forehead. “I’m Eavan Walker, and yes, we are a couple. We became engaged the night before you collapsed. That could be why you're having trouble remembering me."

Simon stared down at their hands, memory slowly filtering back. "No, I remember that. Your Gran took us out to Josh's for dinner. You know, he doesn't do reservations."

She laughed. "We know that. So does she. I have no idea what she was up to that night."

"I think I do." Simon paused, swallowing against the dryness in his throat, sipping from the glass she held for him. "I think she wanted to push us to a decision. Apparently we weren't moving fast enough for her."

Eavan smiled, even as she shook her head. "That would be Gran." She sat once more, releasing Simon's hand. "Ed was by earlier. He'll be back to talk to you. He said they've tracked down who sent the envelope but haven't made an arrest yet. Still investigating, I think was what he said."

Simon nodded. "It takes time to put all the pieces together. They need to have a strong case for an arrest and then for court."

He sighed. "When am I getting out of here?"

"Not for a few days." She shot a look at the door and then brought her gaze back to him. "We need to make some decisions, Simon, and I'm not sure you're ready for that."

"Decisions?" He watched as she frowned at him. "What? No name calling.? No accusing me of being a big oaf?" He smiled as she shook a finger at him.

"There's nothing wrong with your memory," she declared. "Yes, we need to make some decisions. Ed says he needs to keep us together to properly protect us. I just don't see how that can work."

"There is only one way, Eavan, and I'm not sure you're ready for it." Simon watched as she studied his face, comprehension dawning on hers.

"We can't, Simon. We just can't." Panic had begun to set in.

He reached for her hand, tugging her close enough to him that he could wrap an arm around her. "If it means keeping you alive, sweetheart, then yes, we can. I spoke to Jeremiah that night. He was working on getting what we need."

She shook her head, her eyes wide as she stared at him, seeing the confidence he had in her, seeing the love he had for her, and sighed.

"I guess, then. But Simon, what will people say?"

"People will talk. They always do. But our friends and family will understand. They always do. What do we need to do then?"

She finally nodded, her eyes still on his, not turning as she heard the door open behind her.

"Eavan? Samuel's here and needs to speak with both you and Simon." Megan stood at her granddaughter's side, a frown on her face as her eyes shifted between the two in front of her.

"Tell him to come in, Gran. But first, Simon and I have decided not to wait. We'll be married as soon as he's released." Eavan stared at Simon as his head shook. "Yes, when you're released."

"Now that I'm awake, Eavan, they will not let you stay as much as you have. Not as my fiancee. As my wife, yes."

"He's right, love. They've been generous with you up to now, but they do have rules, you know." Megan looked with compassion as the distress colouring Eavan's face before Eavan's stance changed.

"Then, we marry here, Simon. Today. Will Jeremiah have what we need?"

"He will. He would have had it the next day."

Eavan blinked back tears. This was not how she had planned her wedding day, but God was in control, she knew. "Gran, what about my dress?"

"I'll have someone get it for us. I'm sure there's a room here we can get you changed in. Simon, I know you'll want something other than the ridiculous nightwear they give you."

Simon gave a shout of laughter, just as Samuel entered the room, hesitating as he did so.

"Simon? I thought you were sick?" Samuel walked over to shake Simon's hand.

"I am, Samuel, but this is my wedding day as well. Just a small one. Please stay."

Samuel nodded. "I can, I guess. Not what I expected when I walked in here, that's for sure."

Eavan and Megan had moved away, Eavan's phone out to call Maggie, asking her to find a box for them that would be picked up.

"Rings, Gran? What about rings?"

"I sure Simon has already taken care of that. Trust him, love."

Hours later, Eavan wandered around Simon's room, her hands busy tidying vases of flowers that had made their way to him, once word got around that he was awake. They had said nothing about their marriage, preferring to keep it quiet for the moment. Other than to Simon's best friends. They had understood his reasoning but not that they couldn't be there.

Simon finally reached for her hand as he stood on shaking legs beside his bed, drawing her to him.

"Eavan? What is it? It's more than just today, isn't it?"

She nodded. "It is. Here. Sit. You'll fall if you keep standing." She sat beside him, his arm keeping her close to him. "I talked to Ed a bit ago. He's worried, Simon. He said he's more worried than he's ever been. They can't find the men after us. They've gone underground and left no trace."

Simon nodded. "I suspected as much, love. That's what these people will do. I've seen it before, but never felt it personally."

She sighed, her eyes holding fear and panic. "So, what do we do? How do we handle this? I know Gran is safe at Samuel's. He's assured me of that, but what about when she's out on her own?"

"Samuel won't let that happen. He'll make sure someone is with her at all times, until we catch these people."

She finally nodded. "I know that, Simon, in my head. I just don't understand how people can be so evil."

$\mathscr{A}$ week later, Simon moved through Samuel's office building, back at work, but not in the same office. That had been sealed by the police. He sank gratefully into a chair, his strength still not back fully. Samuel watched him, noting the lack of strength and determined he'd send him home early, if he could.

Eavan, Simon knew, was out and about, one of Samuel's men with her. That was a given, Samuel said. She was not on her own, not at all.

"Simon? Any thoughts on what has happened lately?"

Simon looked up as Samuel sank into a chair across from him. "I have some thoughts, not quite organized. Let me run them by you."

Simon began to speak, Samuel pulling paper and pen across the desk to make notes. He was not surprised that Simon had gone right to the heart of the matter and the men involved. That was the kind of person Simon was.

"You're sure about the names?"

Simon nodded. "I am. They are the only two that make sense." He sat back, his eyes on his own notes. "Now what?"

"Now, we start researching harder. These men have gone underground, but I have contacts that I'll use to try and find them." He looked up at the younger man, finding Simon's eyes on him. "I don't have to warn you how dangerous these men are. You know that already. You've had a taste of what they can and will do."

Simon nodded. "I have. My concern is Eavan and Megan."

"We'll work on keeping them as safe as we can. Unfortunately, we can't promise complete protection and safety. You know that only too well, Simon."

Simon sighed, his thoughts on his young bride. "I know. And I hate that." He stared down at the ring on his finger. "I don't think I could handle losing her, Samuel."

"Then we do everything we can to make sure that doesn't happen." Samuel stood. "I couldn't get your paperwork from your old office. I wasn't allowed, but I know you've put a backup in the company safe. I'll get that for you." He walked to the door, turning as he spoke. "You're only here half a day, remember."

Simon shook his head as he grinned, watching Samuel walk away. He knew Eavan would be here to take him home at that point, and he had work to do before she got there.

Eavan stood later that day, watching Simon work away, his concentration fully on the papers on the desk in front of him. She sighed, knowing she would have to rouse him from his work to get him home. The physicians had been really firm about his getting rest, and she intended to make sure he did just that.

A sound roused Simon from his work, and he looked up, his face lighting up as he stood, walking around his desk to Eavan, catching her into his arms.

"Is it that time already, love?"

"It is. Time to get you out of here. Samuel has a car waiting for us out back, he said. He wants to vary where and when we come and go, not be in too much of a routine." She caught his hand, drawing him from his office, but he stopped her.

"I need to lock up what I've been working on before I go. Just a few minutes." He was as good as his word, his work gathered into a neat bundle and tucked away into the safe before he once more reached for her hand.

Eavan wandered their home later that afternoon. Simon had dozed off on the couch and she had covered him with the blanket she had left there. She knew he's be hungry when he woke up, but she just couldn't concentrate on getting a meal ready for them. Megan had left soup in the fridge, telling her granddaughter to heat that for them, it would be sufficient.

Eavan stopped in front of the fireplace, her hand rubbing against the wooden mantle, until she felt it catch on something. She stooped, feeling along the wood again, her eyes following her fingers, until she reached the spot that had stopped her. She felt around the spot and heard a soft click. Now what, she thought, as she lifted at the mantle. Nothing happened. She turned, surprise on her face as she saw an opening beside the fireplace. She walked towards it, hand to her throat, and peeked in. Just a small room, she thought, looking back over her shoulder at Simon. There was no way she was going in there on her own, she thought, and studied the door, finding the way to close it.

Simon was sitting up, watching as she turned, a frown on his face. "What did you find, love?"

"I have no idea. A secret room, I think." She sank down on the couch beside him, her arm going out to wrap around his as her head leaned against his shoulder. "How are you feeling now?"

"Better, I think. Not quite as drowsy but not ready to run a marathon at this point." He nodded towards the door. "Aren't you going to investigate that?"

She shook her head. "No. Not on my own. I think we should leave it for now. I'm worried about you, Simon. You're not yourself, not yet."

He sighed, knowing she was right. "I know I'm not, but what I am is not an invalid." He paused, a thought crossing his mind. "Tomorrow is Sunday. Are you up for church?"

She shrugged. "I guess. I'm not sure though about facing everyone."

"They will all love you, my sweetness. All of them. They have been after me since I moved here to find someone. Some have tried to play matchmaker."

She laughed at that, the musical sound filling the room and his heart. "And that went over well, didn't it?"

He shrugged. "I was waiting for you. God knew." He reached to kiss her, his hand cupping her cheek.

She leaned back, her own hand on the stubble on his cheek. "I'm liking the beard, Mr. Gardner. It suits you."

"It does? And here I was ready to run for a razor and shave it off. I guess I'll have to keep it if my wife likes it."

She shook his head at his grin. "Gran left soup for us, if you're hungry."

He shrugged, his eyes going back to the panel, and he started to rise, falling back to the couch as she pulled him back.

"Not tonight, Simon. Wait at least until tomorrow. I'm afraid of what we'll find and how it will change something in our lives. I can't explain that."

Simon studied her face, seeing the very emotions she was trying to hard to hide. "Never hide how you're feeling from me, sweetheart. That I don't want you to do. Okay, tomorrow it is then. Now, you said something about food."

The next morning, Eavan sat tight to Simon in a pew near the back of the church, her hands clenched tightly together. She had only been in the church a couple of times before, not sure of her reception in town and wanting to avoid those who called her Julia without realizing she wasn't Julia. Simon reached for her hand, his warm and comforting on hers before he heard two little voices coming towards him.

"Are you ready for them, sweetheart?"

She peeked up, a smile on her face as she saw Heidi and Holly heading their way, big smiles on their faces to see their beloved Simon. Heidi climbed on his knee, hugging him tight, leaving Holly standing near his knee, a pout on her face before she turned to Eavan.

"Julia, up." Eavan gave a gasp and then a smile as the little girl reached for her and then hugged her. "Julia, not fair. I want to hug Simon too."

"You'll get your chance." Eavan shared a look with Simon, knowing she had to correct the little one. "But I'm not Julia. My name is Eavan."

"No, Julia." Holly's bottom lip came out in a pout.

"Sorry, honey. I'm really not Julia. See. Our hair is a different colour as are our eyes. Julia's my sister, though."

Holly studied her, the pout disappearing finally. "You not Julia?" When Eavan shook her head, Holly reached to hug her again. ""Nother Julia, can I now hug Simon?"

Eavan started to laugh. "You may be able to, but I'm not 'Nother Julia. It's Eaven."

"That's a funny name." Holly studied her face, her mind working as she tried to process the grown up terms.

Eavan and Simon heard a gasp from beside him and knew Joy had arrived and was about to correct her daughter. Eavan looked up, giving a small shake of her head.

"Let's seen, then, Holly. I'm not Julia, I'm not 'Nother Julia. I'm Eavan. I'm Simon's wife."

"You can't be. I want to marry my Simon." This from Heidi, who had tears welling in her eyes.

Neither woman heard the low words Simon whispered to Heidi, but they saw her reach to hug him and the tears disappear. Eavan turned her attention back to Holly, seeing Joy disappear for a moment, then appear in their pew, to drop into the seat beside her.

"My name's Eavan. Can you say that?"

Holly stared at her, her mouth working as she tried to form the name. "Evie. That's it. Evie."

Her clear voice as she declared her name for Eavan brought laughter and chuckles from those around them, who were delighted to see Eavan with Simon. Simon just knew he'd face questions after church, but right now his attention was on Eavan and Holly, knowing she was handling the little girl just right, not belittling her or talking down to her, but treating her as she should be treated and giving her a choice as to what she did.

Eavan gave a small laugh, seeing Jeremiah on the platform, ready to start the service. "Then, Evie I am. Now, your Daddy's up front, isn't he? Do we have to watch what he's doing?"

"We do. He tells us what to do." Holly squirmed around until she faced the front, her eyes on her Daddy, waiting for him to start talking.

Joy leaned against Eavan's shoulder for a moment. "Thank you. You just handled her like I haven't seen anyone handle her, except for Simon, that is. You'll have to let me know your secret."

Simon stood after the service, watching as Eavan was welcomed by his church family, finally reaching through the crowds to rescue her.

"Thank you, Simon. I couldn't take much more." She walked beside him as he headed for their vehicle.

"I know you couldn't. Listen, I usually head for the B&B for brunch after church. We don't have to, if you'd rather not."

"No, that's fine. I'll have to get used to being around people. I've been hiding for so many years, I'm afraid my conversational skills are rusty." She looked up with a frown as he started laughing. "Now, what did I say?"

"Just thinking about Holly. You handled her just right this morning, Evie." He teased her with the name Holly had chosen.

"That's just for her to use." She gave a pretended sniff of outrage as he shut the door behind her. Once he was behind the wheel, she turned to him. "If you don't mind my asking, what did you say to Heidi?"

He shook his head even as he laughed himself. "I never saw that coming, not for one moment. I just told her that I was already married, that I was too old for her, and that God knew her heart, that He would have someone for her when she was ready."

"Well put, Mr. Gardner. I think I'll keep you and your silver tongue around." Her attention was drawn to the car following them, vaguely hearing Simon's shout of laughter.

Chapter 13

$\mathcal{A}$ week later, Eavan wandered the down town area of Mistletoe, her camera in her hand, being greeted by many of the shop owners. She felt content, loved by a wonderful Christian man, happy to have her Gran loved as well. She stopped as she felt eyes on her and turned, searching for who was watching her and seeing no one. She shuddered, knowing someone was out there, someone who meant her harm.

She stopped in front of Finn's store, finally having made her way to it. She entered, her mouth opening and then closing as she stared around. Here was a treasure trove of photos, she thought, thinking through her client list and knowing just who would want photos from here. She wandered the store, stopping every once in a while to finger a treasure, then move on.

She finally looked up, to find Finn watching her from her from not far away, a grin on her face.

"You made it, finally. I can tell your mind's not on here though."

Eavan shook her head. "I'm not. I have clients who would love to have photos of some of your stock. Can I set up to shoot from here somewhere?"

Finn nodded. "Of course you can. In fact, I'm hiring you to do all new photos for the online store as well. Ann or I have been taking them, but it's time we had a professional do them."

"I would be delighted to do that." Eavan looked around, seeing so much more she wanted to discover. "Unfortunately, I don't have time today to look around as much as I want to. I'm supposed to be heading out to the woods for a shoot, and I'm not at all comfortable about that."

"Who with?"

Eavan pulled out her phone and held it up. "Simon made me get one. Now, let's see." She scrolled through her messages. "Now, that's strange. That message and confirmation for the shoot have disappeared. How can that be?"

Finn froze. "Did you know who it was? I mean, had you met them in person?"

Eavan shook her head. "That's not how my business can work. I often meet up with strangers who book through the website."

Finn shook her head. "Don't do that any more, at least not right now." She saw the fear flit across Eavan's face. "I think it was a set up. The information disappeared because they think they'll have you and that information would lead the police directly to them."

Eavan sank into a chair, her hands to her face. She had set her camera down to look closer at some of the antiquities. "This is what Simon meant, isn't it?"

"I'm not sure what he said, but yes, this is likely what he meant. Whoever is after you will stop at nothing to find you." She looked up with a frown as the door opened and two men entered. In a low voice, she spoke to Eavan. "Take your camera and head quietly for that door at the back. It's unlocked. Lock it behind you. It leads to my brother's apartment. No one is up there right now. You'll be safe. I'll come find you once I can."

"I can't let you do that, Finn." Eavan's hand came out to clutch at Finn's arm.

"You're not letting me do anything. I'm just doing it. Now, go. Quickly." She thrust the camera into Eavan's hands and turned her towards the door, giving her a slight shove that way, before she turned and headed for her office, detouring towards the front of the store as she hit that doorway. Eavan could hear her faint conversation with the men before she quietly closed the door behind her and shoved the old-fashioned bolt into place. She just prayed there was another way out of there.

Simon looked up from his work as he heard Jacob's voice and frowned. As far as he could remember, he was not meeting with Jacob that day. Jacob appeared in his doorway and then dropped down into a chair in front of his desk

"And what brings you here today?" Simon frowned as Jacob just grinned at him.

"What? I can't just stop by and see a friend."

Simon shook his head, his eyes on Jacob's face, seeing that his smile didn't reach his eyes. "Jacob? What is going on?"

Jacob sighed, knowing that Simon had read him just like a book. "Finn called. Eavan had stopped in to look around and they were talking. Eavan mentioned that she had a photo shoot in the woods. That bothered Finn and when she questioned her, Eavan discovered that all contact with the party had disappeared from her phone. Then, two men came into the store, Finn thinks looking for your wife. Finn sent her up to the apartment, making her lock herself up there. She called me when the men had left."

"I don't get it. Where was the man who was to be with her today?" Simon rose, intent on finding Samuel, Jacob at his heels, to find Samuel looking for him, a grim look on his face.

"Simon, we have trouble."

"Where's the man who was with Eavan?"

"Ed just called. They found him unconscious behind Finn's store. He's still out so they can't question him. Where's your wife?"

"Finn had her lock herself in the apartment upstairs to the shop." Simon pulled out his phone, his hand shaking as he called Eavan, his coat in his other hand as he headed for the door, Jacob pointing to his truck, Samuel right behind them

"Simon? What are you calling me for? You're supposed to be working." Eavan's voice held a note of fear but more concern that Simon had called. She wasn't used to him calling during working hours, at least not yet. She would become accustomed to that, she supposed, and look forward to that.

"Eavan, sweetheart. I just wanted to talk to you. Where are you? Did you get to your photo shoot you mentioned?" Simon shook his head at Jacob, who was grinning at him.

"No, I did not." Eavan sounded both angry and disgruntled. "And you know that very well. I suppose Finn called Jacob, who tracked you down, and you're both on your way here." There was silence for a moment. "And yes, Samuel is there as well. How did I do at reading you?"

Simon started to laugh, his fear disappearing at her words. "Just about spot on, I would say. We're outside the store. Go on down and open the door, sweetheart. We'll be inside in just a moment."

Simon headed for the back of the store, a hand raised in a wave to Finn, catching Eavan in his arms as she ran to him, her own clinging to him.

"Where's Samuel's man? Did they hurt him?"

"Knocked him out. He'll be fine, sweetheart. What can you tell me?" He heard steps behind him, and looking over his shoulder, saw Ed and another officer standing there.

"I don't know much. Finn sent me upstairs so she could talk to the men. I don't have the information on the client any more. How did they make that disappear?"

"Let Ed have your phone, sweetheart. He'll let the techs take a look at it and see what they can find out."

She gladly thrust the phone at Ed, her hands shaking as she did so. "I don't want it back. I don't like it." She knew she sounded petulant but didn't care.

"We'll get you another one, sweetheart." Simon's arms were still around her as she spoke with Ed.

He finally turned to Samuel and walked away from Eavan to speak with him.

"I found some more information on her father. He was innocent in all his transactions. That much is clear. I have a call in to the police department where they lived, to see what I can find out about her parents' death. Her father had a heart attack. I want the medical examiner's report on that, so you may have to request that. Her mother had stage IV breast cancer and that took her very quickly, I understand."

Samuel nodded, his eyes on Eavan. "I can do just that. Listen. I'll take what you were working on it, look it over and then lock it away for the night. You need to be with her. That's where you're needed most." He held up a hand as Simon protested. "Trust me, Simon. I can work with what you've given me. She's a priority in the office. Now that Todd's been hurt, it becomes personal for all of us. I have a friend with a security firm. He's sending in people to be with you. You won't see them, but they'll be around you both. And Megan as well, but you know how well that will go over."

Simon chuckled, knowing just how well Gran would take that. "I'll let you be the one to tell her." He turned, his eyes on Eavan. "I'll take her home." Then he stopped. "My car's at the office. Jacob drove us."

"Dan's outside with your car. You left your keys on your desk. He'll drive you home."

Eavan turned as Simon approached, her arms wrapped around herself, before she flung herself at him, burrowing her face against him. This had scared her more than any event in the past, almost as much as what he had gone through. He staggered a bit at her onslaught, then stood, feet apart, as he wrapped her in his arms, his face buried in her hair, not seeing the men and women standing around him, or the customers shooting them curious glances. He finally just scooped her into his arms and headed for the back door, Jacob opening for him, her camera in his hands before he tucked it into Eavan's.

Simon rose from his chair later that evening, his eyes searching for Eavan and not seeing her. He turned, knowing where he find her. Sure enough, she was wrapped in a blanket, curled up in her favourite wicker rocker in the sun room, her Bible open on the table beside her. He didn't say anything, just stooped and gathered her to his heart and sat in her spot, his arms strong and tight around her.

Eavan finally looked up at him, her head tilted back. He kissed her, then raised himself back to look at her.

"Eavan? Talk to me."

She sighed. "What can I say, Simon? Did I bring danger to Finn today?"

He shook his head. "No, I don't think so. She wasn't sure that the men she spotted were after you. She didn't get that reading from them, and she's excellent at reading people. She did see a car circling the block at a slow speed, that she thinks may have been sent there. She provided the plate number to Ed, but it was a stolen plate, so that doesn't help."

She snuggled down further into his arms. "What do we do now, then, love? We can't continue like we are. Someone will be hurt because of us, and that I couldn't handle."

He nodded. "I know, sweetheart. Samuel has called in a friend with a security team and they're watching us and watching Gran as well. He said we wouldn't see them, but they'd be there. They're on you primarily for now."

She shuddered. "That helps but it doesn't solve the problem. How do we stop these men? They won't stop until they're caught. And just how do we do that? I talked to Ed a while ago, while you were napping. He said he's running down some leads, but right now, nothing makes a lot of sense to him or his team. He said it's the same for the detectives on the county force. And Samuel stopped by. He's found out more than Ed has but had to confirm it before he shared it with us. He said some of it you had found earlier today. When I asked him about the secret room, he suggested that we search it, together, and see what it holds. He wants us to do that tomorrow. I had Maggie bring all my cameras here. I can video us as we do just that."

"That's a good idea. Tomorrow morning, we'll go through that room. Maybe by this time tomorrow, it will be all over." He kissed her forehead, before he leaned his head on hers. "I would like it to be. I want to take you to see the tree at night and I just don't want to take a chance."

"We can't stop living our lives. I've heard you've been asked to help provide security on Friday night."

He nodded. "I have been, but I will only help in setting up schedules. My priority is you."

Chapter 14

Eavan drew a deep breath the next morning, her hand tight in Simon's as they stood at the entrance to the secret room, a large-beam flashlight already lighting the room. She entered, staring around, her eyes catching a light switch and reaching for it.

"I didn't expect that." Simon flicked off the flashlight, setting it back outside the room on the floor. He too studied the room, a frown in place.

The room seemed empty, no furniture in it, just shelving with some papers and books on them. Eavan moved around the room, her movement stirring up dust, causing them both to sneeze. She paused as she came to a table, on which rested a large volume.

"What is this, Simon?" She reached for his hand. "What have we found?"

"I don't know, love. Let's see." He brushed at the dust, surprised to see a date for many years ago on the front. "This goes back to the founding of the town. We'll need to open this in front of a lawyer, I think." He picked it up and moved it to the living room, returned to find her packing up the papers and books into boxes she found.

"Eavan, what are you doing?"

"These should likely go to a lawyer as well. I glanced through some. They go back to the founders as well. But there's other stuff as well, more recent. Can we take them to Samuel and have him look after that for us?"

"I'm sure he will. You've taped everything?"

She nodded. "I did. Every speck of dust too." She sneezed again as she looked around. "I don't see that there's anything that we've missed."

"No, I don't think there is." He groaned as his phone chimed and he looked at it. "Samuel. Now how did he know?"

She shrugged as she followed him out, stacking the boxes on the couch as well. "Tell him we need him to come and get these."

Samuel listened as Simon explained what they had found, agreed to come get the material and then arrange for the lawyer handling everything to look it all over. "Did you look at anything at all?"

"No, I didn't. Eavan says she only looked enough to know that we needed a lawyer to go through everything. She has an SD card with the video she took for you as well."

"That's good. She was thinking ahead, wasn't she? I mentioned that but wasn't sure if she had taken that in."

"She did. We'll be here when you get here."

"Good. I have some paperwork for you as well, Simon, from what you were working on yesterday. You both need to see it."

Simon looked up at Eavan after Samuel had come and gone, a thoughtful look on his face. He patted the couch beside him and she finally sat, her hands clasped in her lap.

"What did he bring?" Her voice was barely audible

"I have no idea. I was working on information for your parents yesterday." He raised a hand as she went to protest. "We've already discovered your father was not working for an illegal company, but one of the legitimate ones. We were just looking into his heart attack, to see if there was anything about it that was suspicious." He looked down at the folder in his hand. "Samuel pulled the coroner's report and this is it."

"I can't read it, Simon. You do. Tell me if there is anything about it that we don't already know."

He nodded, his eyes already scanning the report. He finally closed the file with a relieved sigh. "Your father had heart disease all his life, it seems. It ran in his family. Megan never mentioned that?"

"No, but because I'm adopted, it wouldn't have made any different, would it?"

"No, it wouldn't have. Anyway, his heart just gave out. It just stopped beating and they couldn't get it to respond to anything they tried. I'm so sorry, Eavan."

She returned his hug. "It's okay, Simon. I've come to terms with that and with Mom's death. God got me through. God and Gran." She sniffed, blinking back her tears. "What now? Did Samuel have any idea of how long it would take to go through that material?"

Simon shook his head. "The lawyer was waiting at the office, ready to start the preliminary look through. He doesn't seem to think there's a problem. The charter is iron clad and has been proven in court many times. Samuel took a look through the material before he left. He thinks it's just confirmation of what we already know." He paused, a thought coming to his mind. "But how did it end up here? Who put it there?"

"That's the question, isn't it?" Eavan finally rose, heading for the home office. "I have to work on some photos. I have deadlines approaching, Simon. Can I get you anything to eat before I start?"

"No, go ahead, love. I have a conference call in about thirty minutes. I'll take it in the kitchen."

She nodded. "You could use the office. You won't disturb me. I tend to get lost when I'm editing photos."

"No, I think I'll take it out here. Not that it's confidential, but you're too much of a distraction." He waited, a smile lurking in his eyes, for her to respond.

She was at the office door before she spun, his words finally registering. She stared at him, her mouth slightly open, before he grinned at her. She shook her finger at him and smiled, turning once more to the office.

Simon looked up later from his notes as he felt Eavan touch his shoulder on the way by. She had stood for the longest time, watching him work, seeing his concentration, and not wanting to disturb him. She had had an email from Samuel, letting her know he and Miriam were on their way over and had supper with them.

"Simon, Samuel and Miriam will be here shortly. They're bringing us dinner. We'll need to clear either this table or the dining room."

He stood, looking down at his notes. "I'll move to the office. I have about fifteen minutes left to work, then I'm done for the day." He stooped to kiss her, her hand coming up to rest on his shoulder. "Did you get your editing done?"

"I did, surprisingly. All of it and the proofs are off to the clients. They'll let me know in a few days what they want of the proofs. Right now, I'm at a loss as to what I should be doing. I can't put anyone at risk to do any more outside work."

"Then, head to Finn's and work on the photos she wants for her online store. I think that's a great idea. Another line of work for you."

"Thanks a lot," she grumbled. "Did you think I might want to slow down?"

He grinned before kissing her again. "Now that, I can't see you doing."

Samuel finally sat back, wiping his hands on his napkin, a smile on his face as he listened to Miriam and Eavan teasing Simon. He was glad that Simon had found Eavan, she brought out something in him that had lain dormant. Simon finally looked at Samuel, a grin on his face.

"Now, Samuel, as fun as this has been, I think you have news, don't you?"

"I do, Simon. Hold on a sec while I find my file I dropped somewhere in this house." He was up and then back to the kitchen, a folder in his hand, that he handed to Simon. "Read through this and then pass it on to Eavan."

Eavan was having none of that, her chair in her hands as she moved it to rest beside Simon, his arm around her as she sat and they read through the file together. Samuel and Miriam exchanged glances, both thankful for the younger couple in front of them.

"What are you saying with this, Samuel?" Eavan finally looked up. "Does this mean what I think it means?"

"If you're thinking that this means illegal activities are centred in Mistletoe, then you are correct. Somehow or other, you discovered that fact. The photo that you shot, just on the outskirts of town all those years ago, that's the trigger. You didn't realize it was Mistletoe you were at?"

She shook her heard. "No. We were on a trip and someone asked the bus driver to stop near here so we could take some photos. I never knew it was here."

"And somehow or other, they found out you took that photo and have been after you ever since." Samuel shared a long look with Simon before he asked the next question. "When did your father go to work for that company?"

"Around that time." She stopped her words, her eyes finding Simon's, not quite sure what she had just said. Then, the implication hit her and she sobbed. "It's my fault he went there, isn't it? I know I didn't cause his heart attack, but I knew he wasn't happy there and was looking for something else."

Simon gathered her to his heart, his words soothing and calming her, his love and strength communicating to her through his hold. She finally looked up, turning slightly to face Miriam and Samuel.

"Please, tell me it's not my fault."

"It isn't, Eavan. I know your father had been looking for work and took the employment offered him. I've talked to friends of his, who said he felt something off about his employer and was trying to find somewhere else to work. He had done just that, just before he died. He would have started the next week. He wanted to be there, so much, for you, since your mother died."

She nodded, her head going down on Simon's arm. "He was. We were a team, us and Gran. Does she know?"

Samuel shook his head. "Not that we know of. One thing she never told you, and I am breaking a confidence here because you now need to be aware of the fact, she has been receiving the same material that you have, all these years, in an attempt to keep her and you quiet about what you saw."

"She did? She never ever said anything, just made sure I was okay, all these years." She shared a look with Simon. "Now what, Samuel? Now that we know this, where do we go?"

"For you two, you stay under wraps as much as you can. I know Simon has to be downtown during the day on Friday, and that you plan on being there Friday night, but we need to make sure you two are as safe as we can. The security team I called in will stay with you as close as they can. They won't step in unless there is danger that they see. If they do have to step in, do exactly as they as, without any questions. Your lives, and theirs, may well depend on you doing just that."

She nodded. "I understand. Now, about that material we found in the secret room?"

"That, young lady, we're still going over. The journal clarifies and confirms the charter the town set up. The other material, now, that's interesting. It has nothing to do with the town or the charter. In fact, it's all related to criminal activities. Simon, I'm looking into who had the house before you did, and I'm not liking what I'm finding."

"I didn't think you would. I've been tracing previous owners and see the connection with what's been happening to us. I would say that's why they're after me. They think I already found it."

“I would say just that. Now, Miriam, didn’t you bring dessert?   Can we change the topic to something more civil and fun?”

Chapter 15

$\mathcal{S}$imon looked around the town square on the Friday morning, working with the town police to set up the security that had been requested by the artist coming in for a concert. While the artist was not well known, they wanted to protect him as much as they could. Eavan reported that her website had been contacted to do photos of the night, but that she had declined, without any explanation. She just didn't feel safe, she said, and Simon had to agree with her.

He finally stood back near a shop, Ed standing beside him, and looked around, satisfied they had done as much as they could.

"I think we're set, Ed, as much as we can possibly be. There are always unexpected events, but I think we've planned for most of them."

"I think we have. Your expertise has been invaluable. I hope we can continue to use you as a security backup when we need to.”

“I would like that, Ed. This is what I enjoy. That and digging into investigations without having to worry about safety issues. That’s what burnt me out.” Simon shrugged his coat collar up higher. He had forgotten his scarf that morning when he left and was wishing for it now

“Then, we’ll plan on that. See me soon about keeping your weapon certificate on and we’ll do the paperwork we need to to add you as a consultant to our force. Your lieutenant would like to do the same, he said.”

Simon shrugged. “I’m not too sure how much of this I want to do. As long as I can pick and choose, and it doesn’t interfere with my time with Eavan, we’ll be okay.” He turned and shook Ed’s hand. “I’ll see you later than. I’ll do one final check before the concert, which I plan to attend with my wife.”

Ed smiled. “You have no idea how glad we all are to hear you say those two words. We’ve been praying that way for you. You just didn't seem interested in any of the young ladies here in town."

"Yeah, well, there's that. A few were thrown at me by their mothers. That was a delicate situation to extricate myself from."

Ed broke out into laughter, even as he watched Simon walk away. Yes, he thought, Lord, you brought just the right person to him, even if she did call him an oaf at their first meeting. After all, he is tall.

Simon watched as Eavan's eyes widened at the size of the crowd that night. They were standing just outside Josh's restaurant, The House, before entering it. Josh had insisted his friends all join Leah and himself for a meal before the concert

"Is it really this busy, Simon? Does that artist draw that big a crowd?"

He laughed as he held the door open for her. "Not really. But we don't often have concerts in Mistletoe and with the crowds here for the celebrations, it has become bigger than we thought. I need you to stay close to me tonight, or close to the security personnel assigned to us."

Flushed with laughter after the meal, Eavan tucked her hand into Simon's as they walked through the downtown area, skirting those gathered for the festivities. They could hear the sounds of the concert ringing through the air and she was content, more content than she could remember. Her heart sang praise to God for bringing her to Mistletoe and letting her find Simon, or him find her, whichever it was. Gran was happy too, content with the volunteer work she had found and with the friends she had made.

Simon finally stopped, his eyes searching the area, feeling something off. The concert had finished, and the crowds were dispersing. Still, there was something there, or someone, he wasn't quite sure what. He turned to the security personnel who had stopped near them, asking them to watch Eavan for him as he moved away, searching for Ed, needing to speak with him.

Eavan watched as he stood near Ed, who had stopped by the lighted tree, their breath showing white in the air, not too far from where she stood. She burrowed deeper into her coat, glad she had worn her long one. She caught a movement to the side, and squinted, a gasp coming from her as she saw the weapon emerging from an alleyway directly across from Simon, pointed at him.

She screamed his name and ran, the security personnel on her heels as they tried to stop her. She shrugged off their hands and ran faster, her cries to Simon bringing his head around and then he started to turn, just as she threw herself at him. Her assault took them down, Simon stunned for a moment, laying still, not moving even as shouts echoed around them and hands moved to help him sit up.

He sat, one leg still curled under him, one leg straight out as he cradled Eavan to him. He froze, knowing she wasn't moving, her body limp, one arm dangling lifelessly over his, her head on his chest, her hair covering her face.

His hand shook as he desperately pushed at her hair, turning her face to him, her body turning at the same time. He saw the whiteness on her face, that seemed to grow whiter even as he searched it, her lips now with a tinge of blue.

"Eavan? Please, Eavan! Wake up! Eavan? Can you hear me?" His pleas broke the hearts of those near him, seeing that she didn't respond to the anguish in his voice.

He tried to push away the hands that reached for her, but she was taken from him, a stretcher ready to receive her. Paramedics were still on site and hearing the shouts for medics, they had gathered their gear and ran. Eavan's screams had drawn the attention of everyone around them, sending people flying for safety, parents gathering their children close to them.

Ed's hand helped Simon to his feet, his arm across the younger man's shoulders as he stood, anguish in every breath he took, watching as they worked on his young wife.

Murmurs went through the crowd gathered near them as word passed she had been shot, shot trying to protect Simon from his assailant. Officers had scattered but the assailant was gone, disappeared into the crowed with his weapon.

Sudden movement by the paramedics drew Ed's eyes back to them and he watched as they reached to try and stem the flow of blood. Blackie's hands were there, his help needed as they fought for her. He reached for the pressure packings, holding them in place so the other men would work on her The older paramedic had looked up as Blackie dropped beside them, nodding his thanks, knowing Blackie had been in the service as a medic and had seen far worse than this.

Simon watched as they ran leads from a heart monitor, cut away her coat to run IV lines. He cringed as he saw them intubate her, but knew she had to be. His heart cried out with silent tears to God, asking that He spare her. Simon couldn't live without her. He didn't hear the whispered words around him, the doubt that she'd make it to the hospital, the concern for him, the questions of what had happened.

There were murmurs of air transport to a bigger trauma centre, but the paramedics shook their heads, not saying what they thought. Ed realized what they weren't saying, that she would never make it to the hospital in her condition, not to some place further away than just across town. Hands reached to help them load her stretcher into the ambulance, Blackie jumping in, an officer sliding into the front seat.

Ed motioned for an officer to lead the way and watched as red and blue lights flashing, the two vehicles sped away. His arm around Simon still, he turned him to his vehicle, an officer standing ready to slide behind the wheel as they set out.

Simon sat frozen, not comprehending the words spoken to him, his whole being focused on Eavan. He saw the looks that were exchanged, and knew just how much danger his beloved wife was in. He prayed as he had never prayed before. He felt a hand on his and knew somehow it was Eavan's beloved Gran, offering comfort to him, not taking it for herself. He turned his own hand over, clutching hers in his, their unspoken communication one thought, a prayer flowing from both of them for their beloved Eavan.

Doc finally walked towards them, his hair ruffled, blood staining his white coat, his eyes assessing Simon as the younger man stood and went towards him. He frowned. Something was off about Simon, but he just couldn't put his finger on what it was.

"Simon?" Doc's hand came out to hold Simon's arm as he staggered, his feet stumbling over one another. Doc put it down to stress. "We're taking her to surgery now. She was shot, the bullet going right through. We don't know yet how much damage has been done to her abdomen. Jeremiah has called and is on his way in for you. He's set up the prayer team."

Simon nodded. "Will she live, Doc?" His voice was barely above a whisper.

"That's our prayer, Simon. I won't lie to you. We've almost lost her a few times. We do need to find blood for her, but she has a rare type." He looked up at a sound, seeing Julia, Jonathan and Finn all pulling off their coats and heading away with the nurse, Leah running through the outside door, throwing her coat at Josh, as she heard the murmurs that Eavan needed blood. "Simon?"

"Family, Doc. You haven't heard. She's Julia and Jonathan's youngest sister. Someday, I'll have her tell you the story." He looked with a grateful heart as he watched the four disappear, knowing they were going willing, desperate to help save the sister they had just found, a cousin who no one had know about.

The voices around him began to fade as his vision narrowed to a small circle, where everything in that circle moved in slow motion, while everything outside of it sped by. His legs crumpled and he collapsed, his eyes rolling upwards, Jacob and Josh reaching to catch him before he hit the floor. He didn't hear the call for a stretcher, didn't feel them rush him back to a room, didn't feel them cutting away his jacket.

"Doc?" Blackie stood beside his friend, shock on his face. "He was hit? I thought the blood on him was from Eavan."

"I think we all did. We now know where the bullet ended up, don't we? Let's get him assessed and see what we need to do for him. Surgery, likely, as I don't see an exit wound."

Doc stood in the shambles of the room once they had wheeled Simon away, staring at the blood soaked clothing and the debris from treating him. He walked to the doorway of the room across the hall, staring at the same shambles, only many times worse. His thoughts changed to prayers for his young friends.

Three hours later, the group in the surgical waiting room looked up as they heard footsteps approaching them, his friends who hadn't left, her family who wept at the thought of losing her so soon. The men stood, Gran among them, Blackie with his arm around her, as they waited.

The surgeon's eyes searched, finding Gran and coming towards her. She drew in a deep breath, prepared for the worst, as he stood for a moment.

"Doctor?"

"She's alive, Mrs. Walker. She shouldn't be but she is. She's still unconscious and we have her on life support at present. I'll have a nurse come get you in a while, once we've moved her from Recovery. Thankfully, there was not a lot of damage. I expected there to be more, given her presentation downstairs. No organs were touched and even though a main artery was nicked, the work done as soon as it happened saved her." He looked up, his eyes searching the men until he found Blackie. "Blackie, thank you. I'm told your experience helped our men know how to treat her properly. She owes you her life."

Blackie shook his head. "It was a team effort, Doctor. Your men are good." He paused, his eyes searching his friends' faces. "Simon? How is he?"

"He's in a room now. I can take you back to him. Again, the bullet didn't do a lot of damage. It was slowed passing through Eavan's body." He grimaced at the looks of horror he was given from the women, the tightening of the men's faces. "Sorry, folks. I guess when you work in medicine, you think differently about these things that the ordinary person does. Again, he's resting, not a lot of damage. He was awake, asking about Eavan and about Gran. Mrs. Walker, come with me. I'll take you to him."

She hesitated, searching for someone to go with her, and spying Ben standing near them. "Ben, please? Will you go with me?"

He nodded, surprised that she had chosen him, but willing to go see his young friend. He tucked her arm into his elbow, supporting her as she walked, not as spry as she normally did, but with fatigue and worry evident in every step.

The rest stood around, shock still the main emotion, not willing to leave, but not willing to sit. Jeremiah moved from where he had stood, listening to the update, stopping beside each one, an arm around them as he prayed an individual prayer for each one of Simon and Eavan's friends. It would be a long night, he knew, when he finished, and he turned, seeing Samuel standing beside him, reaching to pray for his pastor.

Chapter 16

$\mathscr{F}$ighting against the hands holding him, Simon pleaded with them to let him up, he needed to find Eavan. She wasn't there, and he didn't know where she was. He drifted off, only to wake and try to rise a couple of hours later, fighting with all his strength to get up and his beloved Eavan.

"She's calling for me. I need to find her. She's lost. Please, let me go. Let me find my Eavan." His heart-wrenching words tore at his friends and at the nurses. His voice was low, not much above a whisper, but he poured all his love for his bride into them, his eyes opening and closing as he spoke.

Doc stood there, listening, helping to hold him down before he turned and asked for restraints.

"I'm sorry, Megan. We need to restrain him. If we don't, he'll tear open his incision and he'll be back into surgery.

Even now, I can't guarantee that he won't be there."

Megan nodded, standing back from the bed, Ben beside her, his arm supporting her. "Do what you need to, Doc. We can't have him doing that, now can we? And you said a sedative won't work?"

Doc shook his head. "We can only give so much medication. He's still recovering from that incident a bit ago."

Megan nodded. "Yes, of course. I didn't realize that." She turned, heading for the door. "I'll just go, then, and see how our Eavan is."

Megan paused outside Simon's room, fighting back tears, knowing how close she still was to losing her beloved granddaughter and now Simon. A hand drew her away from the room and to the waiting area, where she was seated and a bottle of water handed to her. She sipped, and looked up, seeing Joy and Jeremiah there.

"You two need to be with your girls."

Joy smiled. "We're here because of them. Both gave us orders to make sure their Simon and Holly's Evie came home soon. How could we not be here, Megan? You're family, you know."

"What's going on with Simon?" Jeremiah turned, his eyes catching sight of Josh walking towards them.

"He's trying to get up, to get to Eavan. They've had to restrain him."

Joy drew in a deep breath even as Josh's hand came down on her shoulder.

"That's sounds about right, Megan. He's the silent one in our group, but there for us all. He would try to get to her, that I know." Josh shared a look with Jeremiah before tilting his head away from the women. "I just need to talk to Jeremiah for a moment. Something's come up that I need his advice about."

Joy's eyes narrowed as she watched the two men walk away, turning as Megan patted her hand.

"Let them go, dear. Now, how are your two girls?" Megan succeeded I distracting Joy.

Josh turned to watch his sister, hesitating for a moment to speak.

"Josh? What is this all about? You said you needed to talk to me."

Josh sighed. "I do. Our group is setting up a prayer meeting starting in a few minutes. I know the church has one going around the clock. We just want to spend our time praying for our friends. I know you can't be there, but we just wanted you to know that."

Jeremiah's smile tightened, knowing the bond the four men shared, having been in the armed forces together, and sharing experiences that no one else had with them.

"That's great, Josh. But that's not all."

Josh shook his head. "No, it's not. Ed talked to me. He's increasing security on both Simon and Eavan. They've received word that someone will make an attempt on one of them while they're in here. He said we wouldn't know who his people were, but that the county force would be sending in officers as well." He looked bleak, knowing this was necessary, before he turned, his eyes finding Simon's room. "I want to stop in for a moment, but I'm not sure I should."

"Go, see him, Josh. You need that reassurance yourself that he's still with us."

Simon's eyes finally flickered open and stayed open, his body sore, his mind fogged. He glanced around, not recognizing where he was, trying to move and feeling the restraints. What did I go and do now, Lord, he asked. Where am I? And where is Eavan? I need to get to her.

He felt a hand on his forehead and then his wrist. He looked around, seeing Leah there, her face concerned as she watched him rouse.

"Leah? Why are you here?" He swallowed hard against the dryness in his mouth and throat.

"I'm here because you need us." She watched as the nurse assessed him, then removed the restraints.

"Why the restraints?"

"Because you fought to get up and we couldn't have you breaking open your incision. You'd have been back in surgery if you had done that."

"Incision? I still don't get it. Where's Eavan?" He tried to sit up, but didn't have the strength to do that.

"You were shot, Simon, three days ago. They had to restrain you two days ago. Eavan was hurt as well." She wasn't the one who should be sharing this, she thought, but God seemed to think she was.

"Eavan? How is she?" He watched as tears gathered in Leah's eyes. "Leah? Tell me, please. Tell me she's still alive." The anguish in his voice caught at her heart and she had to blink hard to fight against the tears.

"She's in the room near here, Simon. She was shot as well. She's getting better, but no one can get in to see her. Not yet. They won't let us."

Simon made himself sit up, his breath catching, his heart pounding, as he gripped the side rails of the bed. "Find me someone, Leah, someone who will take me to her. And now." He held up a hand as he gathered his breath. "If you don't, I'll climb out of this bed and go find her. The consequences of that won't be pretty, I can guarantee you that." He didn't tell Leah that he had been shot before while as an MP. He lived through that and would through this. He just didn't know if he'd live if Eavan didn't.

Leah stared at him, then flung herself to the door, pulling it open, startling the officers standing there, who reached for their weapons. She waved them off, seeking someone to help. Doc was heading her way and she almost ran to him, her words spilling over each other as they walked back towards Simon

Doc stood for a moment, assessing Simon, who was once more laying back, his eyes closed. "He's not going anywhere, Leah. He's asleep this time, not unconscious. We'll get him to her in time."

Doc walked away, stopping for a moment, his hand rubbing down his face. He had not had a lot of sleep in the last few days and it was catching up to him. He paused, his hand on the door to Eavan's room, gathering his thoughts and sending up a prayer that she would be better that morning. The nurses had reported she had had a rough night, and he was almost afraid to enter the room. More surgery was a distinct possibility, he decided, depending on the imaging results.

He paused, his eyes on the young woman who lay, kept alive he thought by all the equipment surrounding her. How could he bring Simon in to that?

He stepped quietly to the bed, his hand reaching for her wrist, his eyes on the monitors, a wonder growing within him. The results were better than he had thought, much better than they should have been. Thank you, Lord, he breathed. No more surgery, I take it. You've stepped in as the Great Physician.

He spoke quietly to the nurse, and she moved to follow his instructions. He had decided to remove the ventilator, to see if Eavan could breath on her own. He waited, his own breath catching as he waited, finally satisfied that she could with just oxygen on her. He inspected her incisions, not finding the redness that had been there the night prior.

The nurse shook her head, a quiet question coming from her.

"It was God, nurse, our Great Physician. She should not have survived before she got here. We almost lost her a number of times down in Emerge and then in surgery. God has a plan for her that He's not sharing. Not just yet. Now, let's see what else we can do for her."

He finally turned, to see Megan standing just inside the door, a hopeful look on her face.

"She's better today, Megan." Doc's voice, though quiet, was jubilant. "She's definitely on the mend. There's a long road ahead of her, but we'll get her better."

Megan nodded, a peaceful look on her face. "I knew she would be, Doc. God told me that in the middle of the night. Now, what do we do about Simon? He needs to see her."

"That he does, and he will. He's asleep right now. Later today, we'll try."

Eavan felt the hand on hers and tried hard to wake up, hearing soft words calling to her. She was too tired, she thought, and slept. Simon watched as she tried to rouse and begged her to wake up, his voice tearing at the hearts of the nurses who stood near him. He bowed his head, his tears falling on their linked hands, before he laid his head down on them, a prayer rising from within that he could not find the words to utter but one he knew had made it to the Father.

Megan turned as Simon was wheeled back to his room, her eyes on him, then rising to the door of her granddaughter's room.   This was not right, she thought. They need to be together, but can't be. Lord, please end this and soon.

Chapter 17

_E_d stood, watching as Simon took in what he had relayed to him. Samuel sat nearby, his eyes on Simon as well.

"So, what you're saying is that you have all the evidence you need to arrest this man, but you can't find him?" At their nods, Simon sighed. "Then, where is he? He could be here in the hospital, just waiting a chance to get to Eavan."

"We know that, Simon. That's why there's extra personnel here. From our force and from the county. We have you under as tight a guard as we can. We have put restrictions in place as to who gets into your rooms."

"I know that, Ed, but they can still get through your defences. Admit that, will you?" At Ed's nod, Simon stared then at Samuel. "Samuel, what about all that paperwork we found?"

"Now, that was interesting, I must say. As you suspected, the journal does go back to the founding fathers. How it ended up in there, no one can say. It does confirm what all we've been told over the years. It is now locked into a safe, and I'm not telling you where. Suffice it to say, that no one can claim property or monies from the trust funds unless they can prove they are direct descendants.

"Now, about that other paperwork. It was really interesting. The lawyer looked through it and immediately handed it off to Ed. It lists crimes, with dates and victims, from the surrounding area and beyond. We need to find this man, Simon, and soon. What he has been involved in is unspeakable."

"Let me guess. Murder. Kidnapping. Assault. Money laundering. Drugs. Human trafficking. Just to name a few crimes." Simon's face was grim.

"You've nailed just about all of them. Except for extortion and blackmail. That's well documented. He tried to get to Josh over The House, but Josh fought back and for some reason, he walked away."

Simon nodded. "I suspect he's been behind everything the four of us have gone through.   Why, that's what we need to determine." He sighed, his fingers plucking at the plastic identification bracelet on his wrist. "Now what, Ed?   How do we catch him?"

"That's what we're working on.   The federal force has become involved as well, since his crimes seem to be spreading out across the country.   He took over the business, shall we say, from his father, and is expanding it, almost too rapidly I would say. We need him, Simon."

Simon sat later lost in thought, after the two men had left, before he turned his wheelchair to the door and set off down the hall to Eavan's room. The staff had gotten used to him making his trek to her room and then staying there for the day, only heading back to his room when he absolutely had to.

Simon's hand reached for Eavan's, feeling the thinness of it and not liking it. He had been informed that she was improving each day, that the medications they had used to sedate her were being weaned from her and that today would be the final day for them.   He wanted her to wake up, to call him her big oaf, to look at him through her beautiful green eyes. Please, Lord, let today be that day, the day she looks at me again. I need that, please, dear Lord.

Eavan struggled against the darkness, her eyes trying to open. She felt a hand on hers and drew comfort from it. Lord, can I just wake up, please? I need to wake up and find someone, but who that someone is, I just can't remember right now. Please, Lord?

She struggled once more to open her eyes, finally succumbing to the blackness once more, not knowing that Simon sat, watching her struggle, his voice low as he spoke with her.

Simon turned as he heard the door open, seeing Ben entering. Ben had become close to Simon over the last week or so, since the younger couple had been in the hospital.

"Ben, what brings you by today?" Simon was puzzled. Ben had stopped by late the night before and told him he wouldn't be around that day.

Ben just shook his head, his finger on his lips, as he approached. "Things have come to a head faster than we thought, boy. We need to get you and Eavan out of here. The doc's working on that plan right now."

Ben and Simon both turned as the door slid open and a man entered, one they didn't know. Simon was puzzled. He should not have been able to get through the officers outside the door.

"Can we help you? I think you have the wrong room."

The man didn't speak, but his eyes narrowed at Simon's words and then he shook his head, a finger going to his lips. Ben moved away from Simon, and Simon wondered at that.

The man pulled a weapon, pointing at Ben, his finger pointing to Simon. "Stay quiet, and you won't get hurt."

Simon started to rise but sat back down as the weapon swung his way. Lord, I have no idea what's going on, but I'm trusting in You.

Ben made a move, and the weapon was brought back to face him, this time discharging, a silencer muting the sound. Ben flew backwards and lay still. Simon sat for a moment, shock coursing through him, before he turned to face the man, seeing another man had entered the room while he wasn't watching.

"So, Gardner, we finally meet. It's been a long time coming."

Simon frowned. He didn't know this man, so why was he here? "I'm sorry. I don't know you. What did you just go and do?"

The man gave a coarse laugh as he sauntered across the room, to stand at the foot of the bed, his eyes on Eavan. "She's the one I'm after. Not you. You're just collateral."

Simon shook his head. "I'm sorry. I don't know what you mean."

"Sure, you do. I've been watching you for years. I brought you and your friends here to Mistletoe. And there's a reason for that. Think hard and it will come to you."

Simon shook his head, his hand resting on Eavan's as she lay, her breath barely audible. He was afraid this was it for them, that they would be dead before long. His attention was caught by the man who had shot Ben, and his eyes narrowed. There was something different about the man, something he was reading but wasn't sure if he was correct.

The man had his eyes on the younger man, not moving an inch from where he stood. Simon shot a look at Ben, laying on the floor, not moving, and frowned. Did he see his chest rise and fall, or was that wistful thinking?

Simon brought his attention back to the man at the foot of the bed, not quite sure where it was going with him. He frowned again, a memory niggled at the back of his mind.

The man turned to Simon, motioning for him to rise. "You're coming with me. I have plans for you, plans that don't include her." He jerked at thumb at Eavan. "I'll leave her to someone else."

The man turned, grasping Simon's arm and savagely yanking him to his feet. Simon was shoved towards the door, his steps stumbling as he fought to find his balance. The man jerked him to a stop, then waited as the other man followed, his weapon trained on Simon.

Simon hesitated at the door, not willing to pull it open, not sure what he would find on the other side, just knowing he wasn't ready to walk away from Eavan. He spun, his elbow coming up and catching the man in the face. He heard bone crunch and the man's howl of pain before he dropped to the floor, his eyes on the man behind him. He froze, not believing his eyes, as the man reached past him and clicked handcuffs on the first man. He shook his head at Simon and pointed silently to the door.

Simon rose, shaking, as he fumbled for the door handle, finally finding it and pulling it open, to fall into the arms of fully geared police, who swarmed into the room, taking the two men into custody. Simon stumbled to Ben, fear in his heart, his hands shaking as he reached for his friend.

He jumped as Ben's eyes opened and he grimaced with pain, his hand reaching for Simon's arm to pull himself upright.

"Ben? I thought you were dead." Simon couldn't express himself the way he wanted to.

"That's what the plan was, son. We wanted him to think that. Else wise it wouldn't have worked." Ben reached for his chest, and then withdrew his hand, seeing the red on it. He gave a grim smile. "Ed and I connected this play, even when I stopped by last night to talk to you. We knew that he was in town and was coming after you."

Simon slid to the floor, his hand on his head. "I don't understand."

"I had to draw him out. He knew I had figured out who he was and he wanted to take me out, as they say. Doc was in on this as well. Eavan was never in any danger. Nor were you, not really." Ben pulled a weapon from behind his back. "I had this and was ready to use it." His hand felt his chest once more. "That hurts, you know." He unbuttoned his shirt, removing it and then the vest underneath it. "I knew these worked. Just never expected it to happen to me."

He stood, reaching down to help Simon to his feet. Simon stood for a moment, his eyes on Ben, before he turned back to the bed, finding Eavan rousing. He blanked out anything around him, his focus solely on her.

Eavan's eyes fluttered open, and she squinted, the glare from the lights strong and blinding. She heard her beloved's voice, felt his lips on her cheek, his hand on hers, and she slept, this time not in a nightmare, but in a peaceful sleep, knowing Simon was alive and well and with her.

Chapter 18

Eavan rested back on the couch, glad to be finally home. Christmas was a few days away, but she was not thinking of that. As far as she was concerned, she had her Christmas already. Simon sat beside her, his arm around her, almost afraid to let her go, afraid that he would still lose her. Doc had warned them Eavan still had weeks of recovery to make, but all things considered, she would recover and be as good as new.

She looked up as Megan rested her hand on her head, before moving on. This had aged my Gran, Eavan thought, before her eyes turned to Ed and Samuel, who sat across from them. Their friends had gathered around them, knowing that this was the day they would find out what it was all about.

Heidi and Holly had climbed up on them, despite their parents' protest. Eavan had insisted the girls join them, knowing how little time they had spent with their father in the last two weeks. Holly had been very vocal that she needed to see her Evie and had handed her a home-made card, bring tears to Eavan's eyes even as she hugged the little girl.

Ed finally cleared his throat, his eyes on the young couple. He had news to share, news that would affect all four of the couples, five, he corrected himself, seeing Jonathan and his Bev there.

"Ed? What can you tell us?" Simon's voice broke through the silence, the anticipation palpable in the air.

"It's a long story, Simon, and we need to go back to the founders. When they set up the charter and the town, they had no idea how many descendants would eventually show up. Some we haven't been able to track down, but most we have. Samuel here has been invaluable, he and his staff, in that. The monies the original settlers put into trust has multiplied many times over, being invested wisely. If you don't mind my saying this, leave it where it is.

"Now, about the last few years. Jacob, you're first, seeing as it was your lawyer who started the process of bringing all of you to this town. He was employed by our suspect, to bring you all to town. We find now that this is unrelated to the town or the charter, but revenge pure and simple. In his twisted mind, he wanted to bring you down and yes, kill you, in a town such as Mistletoe. Why, we're still working through.

"Your lawyer left a statement before he killed himself earlier this year. I'm sorry to tell you that, Jacob, but we haven't spread that word around too far, knowing who we were after.

"Blackie, he brought you here as well. He was planning on you becoming one of the town's paramedics, and would have used that against you. How, we can only speculate, that perhaps he would have caused someone to die on your watch, and you would have been charged.

"Josh, he's the one who arranged for you to appear when you did, suggesting through the lawyer that you might want to take over The House. He was behind the extortion attempts. What all he planned, we still don't know, but it was not likely pretty.

Food poisoning, someone choking on their food and dying, you get my drift?

"Now, Simon. He's the one who suggested your name to the force, dummying up references to start the process. Somehow he planned on having you killed on duty and having a fellow officer charged. You thwarted his plans when you abruptly resigned from the force and he had to change plans in midstream, leading to the confrontation in Eavan's hospital room. Ben knew the man who supposedly killed him. I won't say how or why, as that is a sealed portion of our investigation.

"Now, ladies, it's your turn. Finn, you were never a target. He knew better than to go after you, but through you, he could get to Jacob and tried his best to do so. You overcame every attempt, ones you knew about and the ones you didn't, and there were those. All of you ladies were followed at some point or other and were in danger of being abducted and then likely sent overseas to some country you would never have returned from." He smiled grimly at the shock on their faces, as they turned to stare up at their husbands.

"Julia, he was behind the attempt on your life back in the forest. He was behind it all, Duane was one of his henchman, shall we say? He arranged for everything that happened. He gave approval for your father to be killed, so it wasn't just your mother and stepfather that did that.

"Leah, we have no evidence to show that he was behind Duane's kidnapping of you as a toddler, but he used that to his advantage. He threatened you to keep Duane in line. Donald never knew about his father's working relationship with him. That much we have confirmed.

"Now, Eavan. You're the final one, the one he was really after. He had to do something to get you here, and threatening these ladies and gentlemen were all part and parcel of it. He knew you had a photo of his father you had taken all those years ago, and tried to find it. He threatened you and Megan many times, but you were protected by God, that's all I can say. He was not the one behind your mother leaving when she was expecting you and then putting you up for adoption, but he used that against her. Blackmail was a favourite tool of his. Your biological mother had no choice but to go along with him. Her schemes would have been exposed, and she couldn't have that. He's the one who shot at you and Simon that day, the one behind your incident in the studio, the missing client, the men who showed up at Finn's store."

"But who is he, Ed?" Simon's voice broke through the silence that surrounded them when Ed stopped speaking.

Ed and Samuel shared a look, before Samuel spoke.

"He's someone you know well, the four of you. He was jealous of you and your exemplary service record and wanted to bring you down. He knew he couldn't do it while you were in the service, therefore, he plotted all this for years."

"But that doesn't tell us who it was." Josh spoke up, sharing a look with his three friends.

"When I say his name, I'm sure you'll remember him." Samuel paused at that point, knowing how Blackie would feel about someone he had thought was a friend. "It was Tad Morton."

"Tad?" Shock was in Blackie's voice. "Tad? No wonder he knew how to hurt us."

Josh spoke up. "There was always something about him I never fully trusted. Now I know why. He was always a troublemaker. How many times did you and Simon had to arrest him, Jacob?"

"Too many. He was finally given a dishonourable discharge and we never heard any more about him. When did he take over his father's business, if that's what you can call it?"

"As soon as he returned from the service. There are rumours that he had his father taken down, but we can't prove that. Not yet. Now that he's in jail, we're receiving numerous calls from people that want to speak with us, with information for us about him. We're working through that but it will take time." Ed waited, answering what questions he could before he finally stood, his hand out to shake the hands of the younger men, to give the ladies a hug, before he headed out.

There was silence when he left, as they all looked at one another, before a song was started by Julia and picked up by them all. The words of how God protected and led filled the room, bringing peace and hope to each one.

Late that evening, Simon sat beside Eavan, his arms cradling her to him.

"Do you need anything, love?"

She shook her head. "I have everything I need, right here with you. Gran has taken herself to bed, I think."

"That she has. This was hard on her, you know. We almost lost you. Don't ever do that to me again."

She looked up, a spark of mischief in her eyes. "Do what? Throw myself at my big oaf?"

He laughed. "That and take a bullet for me. I can't handle it if you do that again."

They sat in silence, content, knowing that God had brought them through an adventure they never wanted to repeat.

Epilogue

Simon searched for Eavan just after Christmas, not finding her in the house, or in Gran's apartment. He stood, hands on his hips, trying to think where she would be. He turned as he heard a voice singing from the office and walked that way.

Eavan sat in front of her monitor, her focus on the photos in front of her. How had he missed her, he wondered?

She looked up, delight colouring her face. "You're home, love. Is it that late?"

"No, not late. Samuel sent us all home, told us to take a few days off, that we had worked hard and needed the break. He was planning on doing just that himself." He perched himself on the edge of the desk. "What have you been up to today?"

"Just finishing off some photos for Finn for her online store." She fidgeted with her pen. "There is one thing we need to talk about."

"And that would be?" When she didn't comment, he tilted his head, watching her face.

"Joy approached me. She said because you are so well loved in the community, the church felt slighted that we didn't share our day with them when we married. She has asked if the church can give us a tea or brunch or something like that on Sunday."

He reached to hug her. "I think that's a wonderful idea. I'd like to see you in your dress again. I didn't see much of it before, remember, when I was almost flat on my back."

She grinned. "I know that. I agreed, thinking that it was the least we could do, as a thank you to them". She leaned back. "You do have to arrange for flowers, don't you?"

He shook his head as he hugged her close. "Just a corsage, I think, my love, with a flower matching for me. That will do. If I know Joy and her committee, they've already planned exactly what will be there. We just have to show up." He studied her face. "Are you okay with this?"

She nodded. "I am. I was so lost for so many years, feeling alone, even though I had a Mom and Dad who loved me and Gran who loves me beyond what I ever expected. To have found a brother and sister and cousins has been well beyond my wildest dream. God has been good, Simon. He has given us so many treasures that we will never want for more."

Simon nodded before he kissed her thoroughly. "That I would agree with, sweetheart. He has indeed blessed us in so many ways."

Thank you for choosing to read this book of Simon and Eavan. It finishes off the Mistletoe Treasures series, with Jacob, Blackie, Josh and Simon finding their treasures, their wives.

God provides treasures for us each and every day.   Sometimes we see them. Sometimes we don't. We need to be looking for those, our God moments in our lives. We can be that treasure to someone else. It's just a matter of how much we listen and follow God.

Simon's lady had a mind of her own. I originally planned on calling her Caileigh. She abruptly informed me that was not a suitable name for her, that I was to provide a selection of names for her to choose from. She chose Eavan (Eve-een) which means beautiful in Irish. Ireland has a special place in my heart.   My mother's side is from Northern Ireland and my dream trip is to someday visit that land.

God bless each one of you as you travel through life. Just remember to trust

Him in everything and when things seem the darkest, He is our light.

Blessings.

Ronna